William Livingston Alden

**The Moral Pirates**

William Livingston Alden

**The Moral Pirates**

ISBN/EAN: 9783337178093

Printed in Europe, USA, Canada, Australia, Japan

Cover: Foto ©Andreas Hilbeck / pixelio.de

More available books at **www.hansebooks.com**

# THE MORAL PIRATES

BY

W. L. ALDEN

*ILLUSTRATED*

NEW YORK

HARPER & BROTHERS, FRANKLIN SQUARE

1881

# ILLUSTRATIONS.

# THE MORAL PIRATES.

## CHAPTER I.

"THE truth is, John," said Mr. Wilson to his brother, "I am troubled about my boy. Here it is the first of July, and he can't go back to school until the middle of September. He will be idle all that time, and I'm afraid he'll get into mischief. Now, the other day I found him reading a wretched story about pirates. Why should a son of mine care to read about pirates?"

"Because he's a boy. All boys like piratical stories. I know, when I was a boy, I thought that if I could be either a pirate or a stage-driver I should be perfectly happy. Of course you don't want Harry to read rubbish; but it doesn't follow because a boy reads stories about piracy, that he wants to commit murder and robbery. I didn't want to kill anybody: I wanted to be a moral and benevolent pirate. But here comes Harry across the lawn. What will you give me if I will find something for him to do this summer that will make him forget all about piracy?"

"I only wish you would. Tell me what your plan is."

"Come here a minute, Harry," said Uncle John. "Now own up; do you like books about pirates?"

"Well, yes, uncle, I do."

"So did I when I was your age. I thought it would be the best fun in the world to be a Red Revenger of the Seas."

"Wouldn't it, though!" exclaimed Harry. "I don't mean it would be fun to kill people, and to steal watches, but to have a schooner of your own, and go cruising everywhere, and have storms and—and—hurricanes, you know."

"Why shouldn't you do it this summer?" asked Uncle John. "If you want to cruise in a craft of your own, you shall do it; that is, if your father doesn't object. A schooner would be a little too big for a boy of thirteen; but you and two or three other fellows might make a splendid cruise in a row-boat. You could have a mast and sail, and you could take provisions and things, and cruise from Harlem all the way up into the lakes in the Northern woods. It would be all the same as piracy, except that you would not be committing crimes, and making innocent people wretched."

"Uncle John, it would be just gorgeous! We'd have a gun and a lot of fishing-lines, and we could live on fish and bears. There's bears in the woods, you know."

"You won't find many bears, I'm afraid; but you would have to take a gun, and you might possibly find a wild-cat or two. Who is there that would go with you?"

"Oh, there's Tom Schuyler, and Joe and Jim

Sharpe; and there's Sam M'Grath—though he'd be quarrelling all the time. Maybe Charley Smith's father would let him go. He is a first-rate fellow. You'd ought to see him play base-ball once!"

"Three boys besides yourself would be enough. If you have too many, there will be too much risk of quarrelling. There is one thing you must be sure of —no boy must go who can't swim."

"Oh, all the fellows can swim, except Bill Town. He was pretty near drowned last summer. He'd been bragging about what a stunning swimmer he was, and the boys believed him; so one day one of the fellows shoved him off the float, where we go in swimming at our school, and he thought he was dead for sure. The water was only up to his neck, but he couldn't swim a stroke."

"Well, if you can get three good fellows to go with you—boys that you know are not blackguards, but are the kind of boys that your father would be willing to have you associate with—I'll give you a boat and a tent, and you shall have a better cruise than any pirate ever had; for no real pirate ever found any fun in being a thief and a murderer. You go and see Tom and the Sharpe boys, and tell them about it. I'll see about the boat as soon as you have shipped your crew."

"You are quite sure that your plan is a good one?" asked Mr. Wilson, as the boy vanished, with sparkling eyes, to search for his comrades. "Isn't it very risky to let the boys go off by themselves in a boat. Won't they get drowned?"

"There is always more or less danger in boating," replied Uncle John; "but the boys can swim; and they cannot learn prudence and self-reliance without running some risks. Yes, it is a good plan, I am sure. It will give them plenty of exercise in the open air, and will teach them to like manly, honest sports. You see that the reason Harry likes piratical stories is his natural love of adventure. I venture to predict that if their cruise turns out well, those four boys will think stories of pirates are stupid as well as silly."

So the matter was decided. Harry found that Tom Schuyler and the Sharpe boys were delighted with the plan, and Uncle John soon obtained the consent of Mr. Schuyler and Mr. Sharpe. The boys immediately began to make preparations for the cruise; and Uncle John bought a row-boat, and employed a boat-builder to make such alterations as were necessary to fit his for service.

The boat was what is called a Whitehall row-boat. She was seventeen feet long, and rowed very easily, and she carried a small mast with a spritsail. By Uncle John's orders an air-tight box, made of tin, was fitted into each end of the boat, so that, even if she were to be filled with water, the air in the tin boxes would float her. She was painted white outside, with a narrow blue streak, and dark brown inside. Harry named her the *Whitewing;* and his mother made a beautiful silk signal for her, which was to be carried at the sprit when under sail, and on a small staff at the bow of the boat at other times. For oars there were two pairs of light seven-

THE "WHITEWING" AT HARLEM.

foot sculls, and a pair of ten-foot oars, each of which was to be pulled by a single boy. The rudder was fitted with a yoke and a pair of lines, and the sail was of new and very light canvas. On one side of the boat was a little locker, made to hold a gun; and on the other side were places for fishing-rods and fishing-tackle. When she was brought around to Harlem, and Harry saw her for the first time, he was so overjoyed that he turned two or three hand-springs, bringing up during the last one against a post — an exploit which nearly broke his shin, and induced his uncle to remark that he would never rise to distinction as a Moral Pirate unless he could give up turning hand-springs while on duty.

Harry could row very fairly, for he belonged to a boat-club at school. It was not very much of a club; but then the club-boat was not very much of a boat, being a small, flat-bottomed skiff, which leaked so badly that she could not be kept afloat unless one boy kept constantly at work bailing. However, Harry learned to row in her, and he now found this knowledge very useful. He was anxious to start on the cruise immediately, but his uncle insisted that the crew must first be trained. "I must teach you to sail, and you must teach your crew to row," said Uncle John. "The Department will never consent to let a boat go on a cruise unless her commander and her crew know their duty."

"What's the Department?" asked Harry.

"The Navy Department in the United States service has the whole charge of the Navy, and sends vessels where it pleases. Now, I consider that I represent a Department of Moral Piracy, and I therefore superintend the fitting out of the *Whitewing*. You can't expect moral piracy to flourish unless you respect the Department, and obey its orders."

"All right, uncle," replied Harry. "Of course the Department furnishes stores and everything else for a cruise, doesn't it?"

"I suppose it must," said his uncle, laughing. "I didn't think of that when I proposed to become a department."

The boys met every day at Harlem and practised rowing. Uncle John taught them how to sail the boat, by letting them take her out under sail when there was very little breeze, while he kept close along-side in another boat very much like the *White-wing.* Harry sat in the stern - sheets, holding the yoke-lines. Tom Schuyler, who was fourteen years old, and a boy of more than usual prudence, sat on the nearest thwart and held the sheet, which passed under a cleat without being made fast to it, in his hand. Next came Jim Sharpe, whose business it was to unship the mast when the captain should order sail to be taken in; and on the forward thwart sat Joe Sharpe, who was not quite twelve, and who kept the boat-hook within reach, so as to use it on coming to shore. The boys kept the same positions when rowing, Tom Schuyler being the stroke. Uncle John told them that if every one always had the same seat, and had a particular duty assigned to him, it would prevent confusion and dispute, and greatly increase the safety of the vessel and crew.

2

It was not long before Harry could sail the boat nicely, and the others, by attending closely to Uncle John's lessons, learned almost as much as their young captain.   So far as boat-sailing can be taught in fair weather, Harry was carefully and thoroughly taught in six or seven lessons, and could handle the *White-wing* beautifully;  but the ability to judge of the weather, to tell when it is going to blow, and how the wind will probably shift, can of course be learned only by actual experience.

## CHAPTER II.

WHEN Uncle John announced that the Department was satisfied with the ability of the captain and crew to manage the *White-wing*, the day for sailing was fixed, and the boys laid in their stores. Each one had a fishing-line and hooks, and Harry and Tom each took a fishing-pole — two poles being as many as were needed, since most of the fishing would probably be done with drop-lines. Uncle John lent Harry his double-barrelled gun, and a supply of ammunition. Each boy took a tin plate, a tin cup, knife, fork, and spoon. For cooking purposes, the boat carried a coffee-pot, two tin cake-pans, which could be used as frying-pans as well as for other purposes, and two small tin pails. Harry's mother lent him several large round tin boxes, in which were stored four pounds of coffee, two pounds of sugar, a pound of Indian meal, a large quantity of crackers, some salt, and a little pepper. The rest of the provisions consisted of two cans of soup, two cans of corned-beef, a can of roast-beef, two small cans of devilled chicken, four cans of fresh peaches, a little package of condensed beef for making beef-tea, and a cold boiled ham. The boat was furnished with an **A** tent, four rubber blankets and four woollen blankets, a hatchet, a quantity of spare cordage, a little bull's-eye lantern, which burnt olive-oil, a few copper nails, a pair of pliers, and a small piece of zinc and a little white-lead for mending a leak. Of course there was a bottle of oil for the lantern; and Mrs. Schuyler added a little box of pills and a bottle of "Hamlin's Mixture" as medical stores. The boys wore blue flannel trousers and shirts, and each one carried an extra pair of trousers, and an extra shirt instead of a coat. These, with a few pairs of stockings and two or three handkerchiefs, were all the clothing that they needed, so Uncle John said; though the boys had imagined that they must take at least two complete suits. He showed them that two flannel shirts worn at the same time, one over the other, would be as warm as one shirt and a coat, and that if their clothing became wet, it could be easily dried. "Flannel and the compass are the two things that are indispensable to navigation," said Uncle John: "if flannel shirts had not been invented, Columbus would never have crossed the Atlantic." Perhaps there was a little exaggeration in this; but when we remember that flannel is the only material that is warm in cold weather and cool in hot weather, and that dries almost as soon as it is wrung out and hung in the wind, it is difficult to see how sailors could do without it.

The boys agreed very readily to take with them only what Uncle John advised. Tom Schuyler, however, was very anxious to take a heavy iron vise, which he said could be screwed on the gunwale of the boat, and might prove to be very useful, although he could not say precisely what he expected to use it for.  Joe Sharpe also wanted to take a baseball and bat, but neither the vise nor the ball and bat were taken.

The *Whitewing* started from the foot of East 127th Street, on a Monday morning in the middle of July, at about nine o'clock.  Quite a small crowd of friends were present to see the boys off, and the neat appearance of the boat and her crew attracted the attention of all the idlers along the shore. When all the cargo was stowed, and everything was ready, Uncle John called the boys aside, and said, " Now, boys, you must sign the articles."

" What are articles?" asked all the boys at once.

" They are certain regulations, which every respectable pirate, or any other sailor for that matter, must agree to keep when he joins a ship.  I'll read the articles, and if any of you don't like any one of them say so frankly, for you must not begin a cruise in a dissatisfied state of mind.   Here are the articles:

" 'I. *We, the captain and crew of the* Whitewing,

*promise to decide all disputed questions by the vote of the majority, except questions concerning the management of the boat. The orders of the captain, in all matters connected with the management of the boat, shall be promptly obeyed by the crew.'*

"Now, if anybody thinks that the captain should not have the full control of the boat, let him say so at once. Very likely the captain will make mistakes; but the boat will be safer, even if the crew obeys a wrong order, than it would be if every order should be debated by the crew. You can't hold town-meetings when you are afloat. Harry, I think, understands pretty well how to sail the boat. Will you agree to obey his orders?"

All the boys said they would; and Joe Sharpe added that he thought the captain ought to have the right to put mutineers in irons.

"That, let us hope, will not be necessary," said Uncle John. "Now listen to the second article:

"'II. *We promise not to take corn, apples, or other property without permission of the owner.'*

"You will very likely camp near some field where corn, or potatoes, or something eatable, is growing. Many people think there is no harm in taking a few ears of corn or a half-dozen apples. I want you to remember that to take anything that is not your own, unless you have permission to do so, is stealing. It's an ugly word, but it can't be smoothed over in any way. Do you object to this article?"

Nobody objected to it. "We're moral pirates, Uncle John," said Tom Schuyler, "and we won't disgrace the Department by stealing."

"I know you would not, except through thoughtlessness. Now these are all the articles. I did think of asking you not to quarrel or to use bad language, but I don't believe it is necessary to ask you to make such a promise, and if it were, you probably would not keep it. So, sign the articles, give them to the captain, and take your stations."

The articles were signed. The captain seated himself in the stern-sheets, and took the yoke-lines. The rest took their proper places, and Joe Sharpe held the boat to the dock by the boat-hook. "Are you all ready?" cried Uncle John. "All ready, sir!" answered Harry. "Then give way with your oars! Good-bye, boys, and don't forget to send reports to the Department."

The boat glided away from the shore with Tom and Jim each pulling a pair of sculls. The group on the dock gave the boys a farewell cheer, and in a few moments they were hid from sight by the Third Avenue bridge. The tide was against them, but the day was a cool one for the season, and the boys rowed steadily on in the very best of spirits. There was a light south wind, but, as there were several bridges to pass, Harry thought it best not to set the sail before reaching the Hudson River. It required careful steering to avoid the steamboats, bridge-piles, and small boats; but the *Whitewing* was guided safely, and her signal—a red flag with a white cross—floated gayly at the bow.

Uncle John had made one serious mistake: he had forgotten all about the tide, and never thought of

the difficulty the boys would find in passing Farmersbridge with the tide against them.   They had passed
High Bridge, and had entered a part of the river
with which the boys were not familiar, when Joe
Sharpe suddenly called out, "There's a low bridge
right ahead that we can't pass."   A few more
strokes of the oars enabled Harry to see a long low
bridge, which completely blocked up the river except
at one place, that seemed not much wider than the
boat.   Through this narrow channel the tide was
rushing fiercely, the water heaping itself up in waves
that looked unpleasantly high and rough.   The boat
was rowed as close as possible to the opening under
the bridge; but the current was so strong that the
boys could not row against it, and even if they had
been able to stem it, the channel was too narrow to
permit them to use the oars.

Harry ordered the boat to be rowed up to the
bridge at a place where there was a quiet eddy, and
all the crew went ashore to contrive some way of
overcoming the difficulty.   Presently Harry thought

of a plan. "If we could get the painter under the bridge, we could pull the boat through easy enough if there was nobody in her."

"That's all very well," said Joe, "but how are you going to get the painter through?"

"I know," cried Jim. "Let's take a long piece of rope and drop it in the water the other side of the bridge. The current will float it through, and we can catch it and tie it to the painter."

The plan seemed a good one; and so the boys took a piece of spare rope from the boat, tied a bit of board to one end of it for a float, dropped the float into the water, and held on to the other end of the rope. When the float came in sight below the bridge they caught it with the boat-hook, and, throwing away the piece of board, tied the rope to the painter. "Now let Joe Sharpe get in the bow of the boat, to keep her from running against anything, and we'll haul her right through," exclaimed Harry.

Joe took his place in the bow, and, pushing the boat off, let her float into the current. Then the three other boys pulled on the rope, and were delighted to see the boat glide under the bridge. Suddenly Joe gave a wild yell. "She's sinking, boys!" he cried: "let go the rope, or I'll be drowned!" The boys, terribly frightened, dropped the rope, and in another minute the boat floated back on the current, half full of water, and without Joe. Almost as soon as it came in sight, Harry had thrown off his shoes and jumped into the river.

HARRY SWIMS FOR THE EDDY.

## CHAPTER III.

A S Harry vanished, Joe's head appeared, as he climbed up the side of the bridge and joined his brother and Tom. Their anxiety was now for Harry, who had been swept through the channel under the bridge, and was manfully swimming toward the eddy where the boys had landed. He came ashore none the worse for his bath, and was delighted to find that Joe was not only safe but dry. Joe explained that the boat had drifted against one of the piles of the bridge, and the current and the tow-rope together had forced one of her sides so low down that the water began to pour in. Joe thought that if the river intended to get into the boat, he had better get out; so he sprung up and caught one of the timbers of the bridge, and so climbed safely

up to the roadway.   The boat, relieved of his weight
and freed from the tow - line, drifted quietly away,
and was now floating peacefully on the river about
twenty rods from the shore.

Luckily an old man in a row-boat saw the runaway *Whitewing,* and kindly caught her and brought
her up to the bridge.   As the boys baled her out,
they told him how the accident happened, and the
gruff old man said it "sarved 'em right."   "When
you tow a boat next time," he continued, "you'll
know enough to put all your weight in the stern.
Did you ever see a steamboat towing a row - boat
with a man in the bow ?   If ever you do, you'll see
him going overboard mighty quick.   A boat'll sheer
all over creation if you tow her with a fellow in the
bow.   You just put the biggest of you fellows in
the stern of that there boat, and she'll go through
under the bridge just as steady as a church."

The boys gladly took the old man's advice.   When
the boat was baled out, they floated the rope down
again, and when it was made fast, Tom Schuyler, who

was the heaviest of the boys, offered to sit in the stern. His weight brought the bow of the boat out of the water, and she was towed quickly and safely through. The boys resumed their places as soon as Harry had put on dry clothes, and after a short and easy row glided under the Spuyten Duyvel railway bridge, and found themselves on the broad and placid Hudson. They rowed on for nearly a mile, and then, having found a little sandy cove, ran the boat aground, and went ashore to rest. After a good swim, which all greatly enjoyed, including Harry, who said that his recent bath at Farmersbridge ought not to be counted, since it was more of a duty than a pleasure, they sat down to eat a nice cold lunch of ham sandwiches that Mrs. Wilson had kindly prepared; and when they were no longer hungry, they stretched themselves lazily in the shade.

"Well, boys," said Harry, "we made a big mistake at the bridge; but we learned something, and we won't get the boat swamped that way again."

"I'm awfully obliged to Harry for jumping in af-

3

ter me," said Joe; "but it's the first time I ever heard of a captain jumping over after a sailor. When a sailor falls overboard, the captain just stands on the deck and looks around, kind of careless like, while the second mate and four sailors jump into a boat and pick the man up. That's the way it's done; for I know a fellow that saw a man fall overboard on a steamship, and he said that was how the captain did."

"All right," said Harry; "I won't jump in for you again, Joe. The fact is, boys, I oughtn't to have done it without waiting to find out whether there was really anything the matter with Joe. I'll tell you what we'll do. Joe is a first-rate swimmer, and we'll make a rule that whenever anybody is to jump into the river for anything, Joe shall do it. What do you say?"

"Oh, I'm willing enough," said Joe. "I don't care who jumps as long as the captain don't. It won't look well for the captain to be all the time jumping overboard to pick somebody up."

"A better rule," remarked Tom, "would be that no fellow shall fall overboard."

"I move to amend that," cried Jim, "by forbidding any accidents to happen to any of us."

"But you can't do that," said Tom, who never understood a joke. "Accidents never would happen if people could help themselves."

"Well," said Harry, "if the rest of you will agree not to fall overboard, I'll promise that the captain sha'n't spend all his time in jumping after you. But if you are all ready, we'd better start on. There's a nice little breeze, and we can rest in the boat."

By this time Harry's shirt and trousers, which had been wrung out and hung up on a bush, were perfectly dry. He packed them away with his rubber blanket rolled tightly around them, and Jim attended to the duty of stepping the mast. Then the boys took their places, and Joe pushed the boat off with the boat-hook. The gentle breeze filled the sail, and the *Whitewing* went peacefully on her way up the river.

"Boys," said Harry, presently, "it's getting awfully hot."

"That's because we're sailing right before the wind," said Tom. "We are going just about as fast as the wind goes, and that's the reason why we don't feel it."

"Is this a lecture on wind, by Professor Thomas Schuyler?" asked Joe. "Because if it is, I'd rather hear it when it's cooler. Let's go over to the other side of the river, where we can get in the shade of the Palisades."

It was now about three o'clock, and the sun was very hot. The boat seemed to the boys to creep across the river, and the Palisades seemed to move away just as fast as they approached them. When they finally did come into the shadow of those huge rocks, they thought they had never known anything so delightful as the change from the scorching sunshine to the cool shade. Joe and his brother stretched themselves out, and put their blankets under their heads; presently they grew tired of talking, and in a little while they were fast asleep. Tom was not sleepy; but he was so delighted with the beauty of the shore, as seen from the boat, that he did not care to talk.

For a long time the boat glided stealthily along. The Palisades were passed, and a long pier projecting into the river from the west shore gradually came in sight. When the boat came up with the pier, half a dozen barges lay along-side of it, into which men were sliding enormous cakes of ice. The Sharpe boys woke up, and proposed to stop and get a little ice. The men let them pick up as many small pieces of ice as they could carry, and they went on their way so much refreshed that they chattered away as gayly as possible.

Uncle John had warned them to select a camping-ground long before dark. They remembered this advice, and at about five o'clock they landed on a little low point of land a few miles below the entrance to the Highlands. They first hauled the boat a little way up the beach, so that it would be sure not to float off, and then began to take the tent, the cooking things, and the provisions for supper out of her.

" We want to pitch the tent and make a fire," said Harry, " and somebody ought to get some milk. Let's pitch the tent first."

" I'll do that," said Tom, " while you fellows get the supper."

" It takes two or three fellows to pitch the tent," said Harry; " you can't do it alone."

" I'll undertake to pitch it alone," replied Tom. " One of you can get firewood, one can go for milk, and the other can get out the things for supper. Here goes for the tent."

The tent was furnished with two upright poles and a ridge-pole, each one of which was made in two pieces and joined together with ferules, like a fishing-rod. Tom selected a soft sandy spot close by the water's edge, where he spread out the tent, and pinned down each of the four corners with rough wooden pins, which he cut with the hatchet from a piece of drift-wood. Then he crept under the canvas with the poles. He put one of the upright poles in its place with the end of the ridge-pole over it, and then, holding the other end of the ridge-pole in one hand, he put the second pole in position with his other hand, and pushed the end of the ridge-pole into its proper place. The tent was now pitched; and all that remained to be done was to tighten the four corner pegs and to drive in the other ones.

Meanwhile Jim had taken one of the pails and gone toward a distant farm-house for milk. Joe had collected a pile of firewood, and Harry had lighted the fire and put the other tin pail half full of water to boil over it. By the time the water had boiled, Jim had returned, bringing the milk with him. It did not take long to make coffee; and then the boys sat down on the sand, each with a tin cup of hot coffee at his side, and proceeded to eat a supper of ham sandwiches and cake. It was not the kind of supper that they expected to have on subsequent nights; but Mrs. Wilson's sandwiches and cake had to be eaten in order to keep them from spoiling. After the coffee was gone they each had a cup of cold milk, and then put the rest of it in a shady place to be used for breakfast. The provisions were carefully covered up, so as to protect them in case of rain, and then the beds were made. This last operation was a very easy one, since the sand was soft enough for a mattress, and all that needed to be done was to spread the rubber blankets on the ground as a protection from the damp. Then the boys rolled up their spare clothing for pillows, and, wrapping themselves in their blankets, were soon sound asleep.

# CHAPTER IV.

OME time in the middle of the night Joe Sharpe woke up from a dream that he had fallen into the river, and could not get out. He thought that he had caught hold of the supports of a bridge, and had drawn himself partly out of the water, but that he had not strength enough to drag his legs out, and that, on the contrary, he was slowly sinking back. When he awoke he found that he was very cold, and that his blanket felt particularly heavy. He put his hand down to move the blanket, when, to his great surprise, he found that he was lying with his legs in a pool of water.

Joe instantly shouted to the other boys, and told them to wake up, for it was raining, and the tent was leaking. As each boy woke up he found himself as wet as Joe, and at first all supposed that it was raining heavily. They soon found, however, that no rain-drops were pattering on the outside of the tent, and that the stars were shining through the open flap. "There's water in this tent," said Tom, with the air of having made a grand discovery. "If any of you fellows have been throwing water on me, it was a mean trick," said Jim. All at once an idea struck Harry. "Boys," he exclaimed, "it's the tide! We've got to get out of this place mighty quick, or the tide will wash the tent away."

The boys sprung up, and rushed out of the tent. They had gone to bed at low-tide, and as the tide rose it had gradually invaded the tent. The boat was still safe, but the water had surrounded it, and in a very short time would be deep enough to float it. The tide was still rising, and it was evident that no time should be lost if the tent was to be saved.

Two of the boys hurriedly seized the blankets and other articles which were in the tent, and carried them on to the higher ground; while the other two pulled up the pins, and dragged the tent out of reach of the water. Then they pulled the boat farther up the beach, and, having thus made everything safe, had leisure to discover that they were miserably cold, and that their clothes, from the waist down, were wet through.

Luckily, their spare clothing, which they had used for pillows, was untouched by the water, so that they were able to put on dry shirts and trousers. Their blankets, however, had been thoroughly soaked, and it was too cold to think of sleeping without them. There was nothing to be done but to build a fire, and sit around it until daylight. It was by no means easy to collect firewood in the dark; and as soon as a boy succeeded in getting an armful of drift-wood, he usually stumbled and fell down with it. There was not very much fun in this; but when the fire finally blazed up, and its pleasant warmth conquered the cold night air, the boys began to regain their spirits.

"I wonder what time it is?" said one.

Tom had a watch, but he had forgotten to wind it up for two or three nights, and it had stopped at eight o'clock. The boys were quite sure, however, that they could not have been asleep more than half an hour.

"It's about one o'clock," said Harry, presently.

"I don't believe it's more than nine," said Joe.

"We must have gone into the tent about an hour after sunset," continued Harry, "and the sun sets between six and seven. It was low-tide then, and it's pretty near high-tide now; and since the tide runs up for about six hours, it must be somewhere between twelve and one."

"You're right," exclaimed Jim. "Look at the stars. That bright star over there in the west was just rising when we went to bed."

"You ought to say 'turned in!'" said Joe. "Sailors never go to bed; they always 'turn in.'"

"Well, we can't turn in any more to-night," replied Tom. "What do you say, boys? suppose we have breakfast—it'll pass away the time, and we can have another breakfast by-and-by."

Now that the boys thought of it, they began to feel hungry, for they had had a very light supper. Everybody felt that hot coffee would be very nice; so they all went to work—made coffee, fried a piece of ham, and, with a few slices of bread, made a capital breakfast. They wrung out the wet blankets and clothes, and hung them up by the fire to dry. Then they had to collect more firewood; and gradually the faint light of the dawn became visible, before they really had time to find the task of waiting for daylight tiresome.

They decided that it would not do to start with wet blankets, since they could not dry them in the boat. They therefore continued to keep up a brisk fire, and to watch the blankets closely, in order to see that they did not get scorched. After a time the sun came out bright and hot, and took the drying business in charge. The boys went into the river, and had a nice long swim, and then spent some time in carefully packing everything into the boat. By the time the blankets were dry, and they were ready to start, the tide had fallen so low that the boat was high and dry; and in spite of all their efforts they could not launch her while she was loaded.

"We'll have to take all the things out of her," said Harry.

"It reminds me," remarked Joe, "of Robinson Crusoe that time he built his big canoe, and then couldn't launch it."

"Robinson wasn't very sharp," said Jim. "Why didn't he make a set of rollers, and put them on the boat?"

"Much good rollers would have been," replied Joe. "Wasn't there a hill between the boat and the water? He couldn't roll a heavy boat uphill, could he?"

"He could have made a couple of pulleys, and rigged a rope through them, and then made a windlass, and put the rope round it," argued Jim.

"Yes; and he could have built a steam-engine and a railroad, and dragged the boat down to the shore that way, just about as easy."

"IF YOU WANT TO DIG, DIG.  I DON'T INTEND TO DO ANY MORE
DIGGING."

"He couldn't dig a canal, for he thought about that, and found it would take too much work," said Jim.

"But we can," cried Harry. "If we just scoop out a little sand, we can launch the boat with everything in her!"

The boys liked the idea of a canal; and they each found a large shingle on the beach, and began to dig. They dug for nearly an hour, but the boat was no nearer being launched than when they began. Tom stopped digging, and made a calculation. "It will take about two days of hard work to dig a canal deep enough to float that boat. If you want to dig, dig; I don't intend to do any more digging."

When the other boys considered the matter, they saw that Tom was right, and they gave up the idea of making a canal. It was now about ten o'clock, and they were rather tired and very hungry. A second breakfast was agreed to be necessary, and once more the fire was built up and a meal prepared. Then the boat was unloaded and launched, and the boys, taking off their shoes and rolling up their trou-

4

sers, waded in the water and reloaded her. It was
noon by the sun before they finally had everything
in order and resumed their cruise.

There was no wind, and it was necessary to take
to the oars. The disadvantage of starting at so late
an hour soon became painfully plain. The sun was
so nearly overhead that the heat was almost unbear-
able, and there was not a particle of shade. The
boys had not had a full night's sleep, and had tired
themselves before starting by trying to dig a canal.
Of course the labor of rowing in such circumstances
was very severe; and it was not long before first one
and then another proposed to go ashore and rest in
the shade.

"Hadn't we better keep on till we get into the
Highlands. We can do it in a quarter of an hour,"
said Tom.

As Tom was pulling the stroke oar, and doing
rather more work than any one else, the others
agreed to row on as long as he would row. They
soon reached the entrance to the Highlands, and

landed at the foot of the great hill called St. Anthony's Nose. They were very glad to make the boat fast to a tree that grew close to the water, and to clamber a little way up the hill into the shade.

"What will we do to pass away the time till it gets cooler?" said Harry, after they had rested awhile.

"I can tell you what I'm going to do," said Tom; "I'm going to get some of the sleep that I didn't get last night, and you'd better follow my example."

All the boys at once found that they were sleepy; and, having brought the tent up from the boat, they spread it on the ground for a bed, and presently were sleeping soundly. The mosquitoes came and feasted on them, and the innumerable insects of the summer woods crawled over them, and explored their necks, shirt-sleeves, and trousers-legs, as is the pleasant custom of insects of an inquiring turn of mind.

"What's that?" cried Harry, suddenly sitting up, as the sound of a heavy explosion died away in long, rolling echoes.

"I heard it," said Joe; "it's a cannon. The cadets

up at West Point are firing at a mark with a tremendous big cannon."

"Let's go up and see them," exclaimed Jim. "It's a great deal cooler than it was."

With the natural eagerness of boys to be in the neighborhood of a cannon, they made haste to gather up the tent and carry it to the boat. As they came out from under the thick trees, they saw that the sky in the north was as black as midnight, and that a thunder-storm was close at hand.

"Your cannon, Joe, was a clap of thunder," said Harry. "We're going to get wet again."

"We needn't get wet," said Tom. "If we hurry up we can get the tent pitched and put the things in it, so as to keep them dry."

They worked rapidly, for the rain was approaching fast, but it was not easy to pitch the tent on a side hill. It was done, however, after a fashion; and the blankets and other things that were liable to be injured by the wet were safely under shelter before the storm reached them.

## CHAPTER V.

T was a terrific storm. The wind swept down the river, raising a ridge of white water in its path. The rain came down harder, so the boys thought, than they had ever seen it come down before, and the glare of the lightning and the crash of the thunder were frightful.

"What luck it is that we got the tent pitched in time," exclaimed Joe. "We're as dry and comfortable here as if we were in a house."

"Pick your blankets up quick, boys," cried Harry. "Here's the water coming in under the tent."

Joe had boasted a little too soon. The water running down the side of the hill was making its way in large quantities into the tent. To save their clothes and blankets, the boys had to stand up and hold them in their arms, which was by no means a pleasant occupation, especially as the cold rain-water was bathing their feet.

"It can't last long," remarked Tom. "We're all right if the lightning doesn't strike us."

"Where's the powder?" asked Harry.

"Oh, it's in the flask," replied Joe, "and I've got the flask in my pocket."

"So, if the lightning strikes the tent, we'll all be blown up," exclaimed Harry. "This is getting more and more pleasant."

The boys were not yet at the end of their troubles. The rain had loosened the earth, and the tent-pins, of which only four had been used, were no longer fit to hold the tent. So, while they were talking about the powder, the tent suddenly blew down, upsetting the boys as it fell, and burying them under the wet canvas.

"Lie still, fellows," said Tom, as the other boys tried to wriggle out from under the tent. "We've got to get wet now, anyway; but perhaps, if we stay as we are, we can manage to keep the blankets dry."

The wet tent felt miserably cold as it clung to their heads and shoulders, but the boys kept under it, and held their blankets and spare shirts wrapped tightly in their arms. Luckily the storm was nearly at an end when the tent blew down, and a few moments later the rain ceased, and the crew of the *Whitewing*, in a very damp condition, crept out and congratulated themselves that they had escaped with no worse injury than a wet skin.

"Where are your rubber blankets?" asked Harry, presently.

"Rolled up with the other blankets," answered everybody.

"It won't do to tell when we get home," remarked Harry, "that, instead of using the water-proof blankets to keep ourselves dry, we used ourselves to keep the water-proofs dry. It's the most stupid thing we've done yet; and I'm as bad as anybody else."

"It was a good deal worse to pitch a tent without

digging a trench around it," said Tom.  "If I'd dug a trench two inches deep just back of that tent, not a drop of water would have run into it."

"And I don't think much of the plan of using only four pins to hold a tent down when a hurricane is coming on," said Joe.

"And I think the least said by a fellow who carries two pounds of powder in his pocket in a thunder-storm the better," added Jim.

It took some time to bale the water out of the boat, for the rain and the spray from the river had half-filled it.  But the shower had cooled the air, and the boys were glad to be at work again after their confinement in the tent.  They were soon ready to start; and, rowing easily and steadily, they passed through the Highlands, and reached a nice camping spot on the east bank of the river below Poughkeepsie, before half-past five.

This time they selected a place to pitch the tent with great care.  It was easy to find the high-water mark on the shore, and the tent was pitched a little above it, so as to be safe from a disaster like that of the previous night. Harry wanted it pitched on the top of a high bank; but the others insisted that, as long as they were safe from the tide, there was no need of putting the tent a long distance from the water, and that they had selected the only spot where they could have a bed of sand to sleep on.

This important business being settled, supper was the next subject of attention.

"We haven't been as regular about our meals as we ought to be," said Harry, "but it hasn't been our fault. We'll have a good supper to-night, at any rate. How would you like some hot turtle-soup?"

"Just the thing," said Joe. "The bread is beginning to get a little dry; but we can soak it in the soup."

"About going for milk," continued Harry; "we ought to arrange that and the other regular duties. Suppose after this we take regular turns. One fellow can pitch the tent, another can go for milk, another can get the firewood, and the other can cook.

We can arrange it according to alphabetical order. For instance, Tom Schuyler pitches the tent to-night; Jim Sharpe goes for milk, Joe gets the firewood, and I cook. The next time we camp, Jim will pitch the tent, Joe will get the milk, I will get the wood, and Tom will cook. Is that fair?"

The boys said it was, and they agreed to adopt Harry's proposal. Jim went off with the milk-pail, and when the fire was ready, Harry took a can of soup and put it on the coals to be heated.

Jim found a house quite near at hand, where he bought two quarts of milk and a loaf of bread, and was back again at the camp before the soup was ready. He found the boys lying near the fire, wait-ing for the soup to heat and the coffee to boil.

"That soup takes a long time to heat through," said Tom. "There isn't a bit of steam coming out of it yet."

"How can any steam come out of it when it's sol-dered up tight," replied Harry.

"You don't mean to tell me that you've put the

THE SOUP EXPLOSION.

can on the fire without punching a hole in the top?"

"Of course I have. What on earth should I punch a hole in it for?"

"Because—" cried Tom, hastily springing up.

But he was interrupted by a report like that of a small cannon: a cloud of ashes rose over the fire, and a shower of soup fell just where Tom had been lying.

"That's the reason why," resumed Tom. "The steam has burst the can, and the soup has gone up."

"We've got another can," said Harry, "and we'll punch a hole in that one. What an idiot I was not to think of its bursting! It's a good job that it didn't hurt us. I should hate to have the newspapers say that we had been blown up and awfully mangled with soup."

The other can of soup was safely heated, and the boys made a comfortable supper. They drove a stake in the sand, and fastened the boat's painter securely to it, and then "turned in."

"No tide to rouse us up to-night, boys," said Harry, as he rolled himself in his blanket. "I sha'n't wake up till daylight."

"We'd better take an early start," remarked Tom. "We haven't got on very far because we started so late this morning. If we get off by six every morning, we can lie off in the middle of the day, and start again about three o'clock. It's no fun rowing with the sun right overhead."

"Well, it isn't more than eight o'clock now; and, if we take eight hours' sleep, we can turn out at four o'clock," said Harry. "But who is going to wake us up? Joe and Jim are sound asleep already, and I'm awful sleepy myself. I don't believe one of us will wake up before seven o'clock anyway."

Tom made no answer, for he had dropped asleep while Harry was talking. The latter thought he must be pretending to sleep, and was just resolving to tell Tom that it wasn't very polite to refuse to answer a civil question, when he found himself muttering something about a game of base-ball, and awoke, with a start, to discover that he could not possibly keep awake another moment.

The boys slept on. The moon came out and shone in at the open tent-flap, and the tide rose to high-water mark, but not quite high enough to reach the tent. By-and-by the wheezing of a tow-boat broke the stillness, and occasionally a hoarse steam-whistle echoed among the hills; but the boys slept so soundly that they would not have heard a loco-motive had it whistled its worst within a rod of the tent.

The river had been like a mill-pond since the thunder-storm, but about midnight a heavy swell rolled in toward the shore. It came on, growing larger and larger, and, rushing up the little beach with a fierce roar, dashed into the tent and over-whelmed the sleeping boys without the slightest warning.

## CHAPTER VI.

THE wave receded as suddenly as it came. The boys sprang up in a terrible fright, and indeed there are few men who in their place would not have been frightened. The shock of the cold water was enough to startle the strongest nerves, and as the boys rushed to the door of the tent, in a blind race for life, they fully believed that their last hour had come. Before they could get out of the tent, a second wave swept up and rose above their knees. With wild cries of terror the two younger boys caught hold of Tom, and, losing their footing, dragged him down. Harry caught at Tom impulsively, with a vague idea of saving him from drowning, but the only result of his effort was that he went down with the rest. Fortunately the wave receded before the boys had time to drown, and left them struggling in a heap on the wet sand. There was no return of the water, and in a few moments the boys were outside of the tent and on the top of the bluff above the river.

"It must have been a tidal wave," said Jim. "Oh, I'd give anything if I was home! The water will come up again, and we'll all be drowned!"

"It was the swell of a steamboat," said Tom. "There's the boat now, just going around that point."

"You're right," said Harry. "It was nothing but the swell of the night-boat. What precious fools we were not to think of it before! To-morrow night we'll pitch the tent about a thousand feet above the water."

"Then there'll be a water-spout or something," said Jim. "We're bound to get wet whatever we do. We only started yesterday, and here we've been wet through three times."

"And Harry has been wet four times, counting

5

the time he jumped in the Harlem for me," added
Joe.

"It won't do to stand here and talk about it," said
Tom.    "We've got to have a fire or we'll freeze to
death.    Look at the way Joe's teeth are chattering.
The blankets and clothes are all wet, and the sooner
we dry them the sooner we'll get warm."

There happened to be a dead tree near by, and it
was soon converted into firewood.    The boys built
a roaring fire on a large flat rock, and after it had
burnt for a little while they pushed it about six
feet from the place where they had started it, and,
after piling fresh fuel on it, laid down on the hot
rock with their feet to the flames.    The fire had
heated the rock so that they could hardly bear to
touch it, but the heat dried their wet clothes rapidly,
and kept them from taking severe colds.    Meanwhile
their blankets had been spread out near the fire,
and in half an hour were very nearly dry, and pretty
severely scorched.    Two large logs were then rolled
on the fire, and when they were in a blaze the

THE BOYS BUILT A ROARING FIRE ON A LARGE FLAT ROCK.

boys wrapped themselves in their blankets, and, lying as near to the fire as they could without actually burning, resumed their interrupted sleep. They found the rock rather a hard bed, and it offered no temptation to laziness; so it happened that they were all broad awake at half-past four; and though somewhat stiff from lying on a rocky bed, were none the worse for their night's adventure.

"There's one thing I'm going to do this very day," said Harry, as they were dressing themselves after their morning swim. "I'm going to write to the Department to send us a big rubber bag, that we can put our spare clothes in and keep them dry. There's no fun in being wet and having nothing dry to put on."

"If we have the bag sent to Albany, it will get there by the time we do," said Tom. "You write the letter while we are getting breakfast."

So Harry wrote to the Department as follows:

"DEAR UNCLE JOHN,—We've been wet through with a steamboat once, and the tide wet us the first night, and we got rained on, and I jumped in to get Joe out, and we've had a gorgeous time. Please send us a big water-proof bag to put our spare clothes in, so that we can have something dry. Please send it to Albany, and we will stop there at the post-office for it. Please send it right away. You said the Department furnished everything. We've been dry twice since we started, but it didn't last long. There never was such fun. All the boys send their love to you. Please don't forget the bag. From your affectionate nephew,

"HARRY."

"This was the morning that you were going to sleep till eight o'clock without waking up, Harry," said Tom, as they were eating their breakfast.

"There's nothing that will wake a fellow up so quick as the Hudson River rolling in on him. I hadn't expected to wake up in that way," answered Harry.

"So far we have done nothing but find out how stupid we are," said Tom. "Seems to me we must have found it pretty near all out by this time. There can't be many more stupid things that we haven't done."

"There won't any accident happen to-night," replied Harry; "for I'll make sure that the tent is pitched so far from the water that we can't be wet again. I wonder if every fellow learns to camp out by getting into scrapes as we do. It is very certain that we won't forget what we learn on this cruise."

"I'm beginning to get tired of ham," exclaimed Joe. "We've been eating ham ever since we started. Let's get some eggs to-day."

"And some raspberries," suggested Jim. "It's the season for them."

"And let's catch some fish," said Tom.

"That's what we'll do," said Harry. "We'll sail till eleven o'clock, and then we'll go fishing and catch our dinner."

This suggestion pleased everybody; and when, at about six o'clock, they set sail with a nice breeze from the south, everybody kept a lookout for a good fishing-ground, and wondered why they had not thought of fishing before.

## CHAPTER VII.

THE sun was getting to be rather too hot for boating when the boys saw the half-sunken wreck of a canal-boat close to the west shore, where there was a nice shady grove. They immediately crossed the river, and, landing near the wreck, began to get their fishing-tackle in order.

As there were only two poles, one of which belonged to Harry, and the other to Tom, the two Sharpe boys were obliged either to cut poles for themselves, or to watch the others while they fished. Jim cut a pole for himself, but Joe preferred to lie on the bank. "I don't care to fish, anyhow," he said. "I'll agree to eat twice as much fish as anybody else, if I can be excused from fishing."

"If you don't want to fish, you'd better hunt bait for us," said Tom.

"I never thought about bait," exclaimed Harry. "How are we going to dig for worms without a spade?"

"Who wants any worms?" replied Tom. "Grasshoppers are the thing; and the field just back of here is full of them. Come, Joe, catch us some grasshoppers, won't you?"

"How many do you want?" asked Joe. "I don't want to waste good grasshoppers on fellows who won't use them. Let's see: suppose I get you ten grasshoppers apiece. Will that do?"

"Are you getting lazy, Joe?" said Tom, "or are you sick? A fellow who don't want to fish must have something wrong in his insides. Harry, you'd better give him some medicine."

"Oh, I'm all right," replied Joe. "I'm a little sleepy to-day, but I'll get your grasshoppers."

Joe took an empty tin can and went in search of grasshoppers, while the rest were getting their hooks and lines ready. In a short time he returned, and handed the can to Tom. "There's just thirty-one grasshoppers in that can," said he. "I threw in one for good measure. Now go ahead and fish, and I'll have a nap." So saying, he stretched himself on the ground, and the other boys began to fish.

There were quantities of perch near the old canal-boat, and they bit ravenously at the grasshoppers. It took only about a quarter of an hour to catch nearly three dozen fish. These were more than the boys could possibly eat; and Tom was just going to remark that they had better stop fishing, when they were startled by a loud cry from Joe. Harry, in swinging his line over his head so as to cast out a long way into the river, had succeeded in hooking Joe in the right ear.

Of course Harry was extremely sorry, and he said so several times; but, as Joe pointed out, "talk won't pull a hook out of a fellow's ear!" The barb made it impracticable to draw the hook out, and it was quite impossible that Joe should enjoy the cruise with a fish-hook in his ear. Jim said that the hook must be cut out; but Joe objected to having his ear cut

JOE IS CAUGHT.

to pieces with a dull jack-knife. In this emergency Tom proposed to break off the shank of the hook, and then to push the remainder of it through the ear. It was no easy matter, however, to break the steel. Every time the hook was touched, Joe winced with pain; but finally Tom managed to break the shank with the aid of the pair of pliers that formed part of the stores. The hook was then gently and firmly pressed through the ear, and carefully drawn out.

"I knew," said Tom, "that something must be wrong when Joe said he didn't want to fish. This ought to be a warning to him."

"It's a warning to me," said Harry, "not to throw my line all over the State of New York."

"Oh, it's all right now," said Joe. "Only the next time I go cruising with Harry, I'm going to take a pair of cutting pincers to cut off the shanks of fish-hooks after he gets through fishing. We'd better get a pair at Hudson, anyhow, or else we'll all be stuck full of hooks, if Harry does any more fishing."

Harry was so humbled by the result of his care-
lessness that he offered, by way of penance, to clean
and cook the fish. When this was done, and the
fish were served up smoking hot, they were so good
that Joe forgot his damaged ear, and Harry recover-
ed his spirits. After a course of fish and bread, a
can of peaches was opened for dessert, and then followed a good long rest. By three o'clock the heat
began to lessen, and the *Whitewing* started on her
way with a better breeze than she had yet been fa-
vored with.

The boat travelled swiftly, and the breeze gradually freshened. The whitecaps were beginning to
make their appearance on the river before it occurred to the boys that they must cross over to the east
shore, in order to camp where they could find shade
while getting breakfast the next morning. It had
been one of Uncle John's most earnest bits of advice
that they should always have shade in the morning.
" Nothing spoils the temper," he had said, " like cooking under a bright sun ; so make sure that you keep

in the shade until after breakfast." Harry felt a little nervous about crossing the river in so fresh a
breeze, since, as the breeze blew from the south, the
boat could not sail directly across the river without
bringing the sea on her beam. He did not mention
that he was nervous, however, and he showed excel-
lent judgment in crossing the river diagonally, so as
to avoid exposing the broadside of the boat to the
waves, that by this time were unpleasantly high.
The east bank was thus reached without taking a
drop of water into the boat, and she was then kept
on her course up the river, within a few rods of the
shore.

This was a wise precaution in one respect; for, if
the boat had capsized, the boys could easily have
swum ashore; but still it is always risky to keep
close to the shore, unless you know that there are no
rocks or snags in the way. Harry never thought
of the danger of being shipwrecked with the shore
so close at hand, and was enjoying the cooling breeze
and the speed of the boat, when suddenly the *White-*

*wing* brought up with a crash that pitched everybody into the bottom of the boat.  She had struck
a sunken rock, and the speed at which she was going
was so great that one of her planks was stove in.
Before the boys could pick themselves up, the water
had rushed in, and was rising rapidly.  "Jump overboard, everybody!" cried Harry.  "She won't float
with us in her."  There was no time in which to
pull off shirts and trousers, and the boys plunged
overboard without even taking their hats off.  They
then took hold of the boat, two on each side of her,
and swam toward the shore.  With so much water
in her, the boat was tremendously heavy; but the
boys persevered, and finally reached shallow water,
where they could wade and drag her out on the sand.

"Here we are wet again!" exclaimed Jim.  "The
blankets are wet, too, this time."

"Never mind," replied Tom.  "It's not more
than five o'clock, and we can get them dry before
night."

"We'll have to work pretty fast, then," said Harry. "Jim and Joe had better build a big fire and dry the things, while you and I empty the boat; or I'll empty the boat, and you can pitch the tent. We'll have to put off supper till we can make sure of a dry bed."

Harry took the things out of the boat one by one. Everything was wet except the contents of the tin boxes, into which the water luckily had not penetrated. As soon as the fire was built, Jim and Joe gave their whole attention to drying the blankets and the spare clothing; and when the boat was emptied, it was found that a hole nearly six inches long and four inches wide had been made through one of the bottom planks. Harry and Tom set to work to mend it. They took a piece of canvas—which had luckily been kept in one of the tin boxes and was quite dry—and tacked it neatly over the outside of the hole. They next covered the canvas with a thin coating of white-lead, except at the edges, where the white-lead was laid on very thickly. Over the canvas the piece of zinc that had been

6

brought for just such a purpose was carefully tacked, and then thin strips of wood were placed over
the edges of the tin, and screwed down tightly with
screws that went through the zinc, but not through
the canvas. Finally, white-lead was put all around
the outer edge of the zinc, and the boat was then
left bottom-side up on the sand, so that the white-
lead could harden by exposure to the air.

Nobody cared to go for milk in wet clothes; and
so, when the boat was mended, the boys all sat
around the fire to dry themselves, and made a supper of crackers. What with the heat and the wind,
it was not very long before their clothes and blankets were thoroughly dried; and they could look forward to a comfortable night. The tent was pitched
where no steamboat swell could possibly touch it,
and the boat was apparently out of reach of the tide.
It was very early when the boys "turned in," and
for the first time in the cruise they slept peacefully
all night.

## CHAPTER VIII.

THE next morning the boys awoke early, having had a thoroughly good night's rest. Tom, whose turn it was to go for milk, found a well-stocked farm-house, where he obtained not only milk, bread, and eggs, but a supply of butter and a chicken all ready for cooking. After breakfast the boat was put in the water, and, to the delight of all, proved to be almost as tight as she was before running into the rock. A little water came in at first under the edges of the zinc, but in a short time the wood swelled, and the leak entirely ceased.

The boat was loaded, and the boys were ready to start soon after six o'clock. There was no wind, but the two long oars, pulled one by Tom and the other by Jim, sent her along at a fine rate. They rowed until ten o'clock, resting occasionally for a few moments, and then, as there were no signs of a breeze, and as it was growing excessively hot, they went ashore, to wait until afternoon before resuming their journey.

The sun became hotter and hotter. The boys tried to fish, but there was no shade near the bank of the river, and it was too hot to stand or sit in the sunshine and wait for fish to bite. They went in swimming, but the sun, beating on their heads, seemed hotter while they were in the water than it did when they were on the land. Jim and Joe tried a game of mumble-to-peg, but they gave it up long before they had reached "ears." It was probably the hottest day of the year; and as it was clearly impossible to row or to do anything else while the heat lasted, the boys brought their blankets from the boat, and, going to a grove not far from the shore, lay down and fell asleep.

They were astonished to find, when they awoke, that it was two o'clock. None of them had been ac-

MUMBLE-THE-PEG.

customed to sleep in the daytime, and they could not understand how it came about that they had all slept for fully two hours. They had yet to learn that one of the results of "camping out," or living in the open air, is an ability to sleep at almost any time. All animals and wild creatures, whether they are beasts or savages, have this happy faculty of sleeping in the daytime. It is one of the habits of our savage ancestors that comes back to us when we abandon civilization, and live as Aryan tribes, from whom we are descended, lived in the Far East, before they marched with their wives and children and cattle from India, and made themselves new homes in Europe.

After lunch the boys prepared to start, although there was still no wind; but when they went down to the boat they found that the sun was as hot as ever. So they returned to the shade of the grove, and made up their minds to stay there until the end of the afternoon.

"Harry," said Tom, "we've been on the river

three days, and we are only a little way above Hudson. How much longer will it be before we get to Albany?"

"We ought to get there in two days more, even if we have to row all the way," replied Harry.

"And after we get to Albany, what are we to do next?"

"We are going up the Champlain Canal to Fort Edward. There we will have a wagon to carry us and the boat to Warrensburg, on the Schroon River, and will go up the river to Schroon Lake. Uncle John laid out the route for us."

"How many days will it take us to get to the lake?" asked Tom.

Harry thought awhile. "There's two days more on the Hudson, two on the canal, and maybe two on the Schroon River. And then there's a Sunday, which don't count. It'll be just a week before we get to the lake."

"I've got to be home by two weeks from next Monday," continued Tom, "so I sha'n't have much time on the lake. Can't we get along a little faster? There's a full-moon to-night, and suppose we sail all night—or row, if the wind doesn't come up."

"That's a first-rate idea," exclaimed Harry. "We can take turns sleeping in the bottom of the boat. Why, if the breeze comes up in the night, we might make twenty or thirty miles before morning."

All the boys liked the plan of sailing at night, and they resolved to adopt it. While they were yet discussing it, a light breeze sprang up, from the south as usual, and they hastened to take advantage of it. In the course of an hour more the sun began to lose its power; and when they went ashore at six o'clock to cook their supper, they had sailed about fifteen miles.

As they expected to make so much progress during the night, they were in no hurry about supper, and it was not until after seven o'clock that they again made sail. Harry divided the crew into watches—one consisting of himself and Joe Sharpe, and the other of Tom and Jim. Each watch was to have charge of the boat for three hours, while the other watch slept. At eight o'clock Tom and Jim lay down in the bottom of the boat, and Joe came aft to take Tom's customary place at the sheet. Harry, of course, steered.

All went well. The breeze was light but steady, and Harry kept the boat in the middle of the river to avoid another shipwreck. The watch below did not sleep much, for they had had a long nap at noon, and, besides, the novelty of their position made them wakeful. They had just dropped asleep when eleven o'clock arrived, and they were awakened to relieve the other watch. Tom went sleepily to the helm, and Harry and Joe gladly "turned in," and were soon fast asleep.

Tom always declares that he never closed his eyes while he was at the helm, and Jim also asserts that he was wide awake during his entire watch, though neither he nor Tom spoke for fear of waking up the other boys. It was strange that these two wide-awake young Moral Pirates did not notice that a large steamboat—one of the Albany night-boats—was in sight, until she was within a mile of them, and it is just possible that, without knowing it, they were a little too drowsy to keep a proper lookout.

As soon as Tom saw the steamboat, he remarked, "Halloo! there's one of the Albany boats," and steered the boat over toward the east shore. The breeze had nearly died away, and the *Whitewing* moved very slowly. The steamboat came rapidly down the river, her paddles throbbing loudly in the night air. Jim began to get a little uneasy, and said, "I hope she won't run us down." "Oh, there's no danger!" replied Tom; "we shall get out of her way easy enough." But, to his dismay, the steamboat, instead of keeping in the middle of the river, presently turned toward the east shore, as if she were bent upon running down the *Whitewing*. Tom was now really alarmed; and as he saw that the sail was doing very little good, he hurriedly told Jim to take down the mast and get out the oars as quick as possible. Jim rapidly obeyed the order, dropping the mast on Harry's head, and catching Joe by the nose in his search for the oars. By this time Tom had begun to hail the steamboat at the top of his lungs; but no attention was paid to him by the steamboat men, since the noise of the paddles drowned Tom's voice. Harry and Joe, who were now wide awake, saw what danger they were in, and they sprang to the oars. The steamboat was frightfully near, and still hugging the shore; but Tom called on the boys to give way with their oars, and steered straight for the shore, knowing that there must be room for the boat between the steamboat and the bank of the river, and fearing that if he steered in the opposite direction the steamboat might change her course and run them down, when they would have little chance of escape by swimming.

It was certainly very doubtful if they could avoid the steamboat, and Tom was well aware of it. He told the other boys that, if they were sure to be run down, they must jump before the steamboat struck them, and dive, so as to escape the paddles. "I'll tell you when to jump, if worst comes to worst," said he; "but don't you look around now, nor do anything but row. Row for your lives, boys." And the boys did row gallantly. Harry had a pair of sculls, and Jim had a long oar, and between them they made the boat fly through the water. As they neared the shore, it seemed to them that there was not more than three feet of space between the steamboat and the land; and Tom had almost made up his mind that the cruise was coming to a sudden end, when the great steamboat swung her head around, and drew out toward the middle of the river. She did not seem to be more than a rod from them as she changed her course, though in reality she was probably much farther off. At the same moment the *Whitewing* reached what appeared to be the shore, but what was really a long row of piles projecting about a foot above the water. The boys had just ceased rowing, and Tom had given the boat a sheer with the rudder, so as to bring her along-side of the piles, when the steamboat's swell, which the boys, in their

excitement over their narrow escape, had totally forgotten, came rushing up, seized the boat, and threw
it over the piles into a shallow and muddy lagoon.

It was almost miraculous that the boat was not
capsized; but she was actually lifted up and thrown
over the piles, without taking more than a few quarts
of spray into her. When they saw that they were
absolutely safe, the boys began to wonder how in
the world they could get the boat back into the
river, and Jim proposed to light the lantern and see
if anything was missing out of the boat, and if she
had been injured.

"Now I see why the steamboat did not notice us,"
exclaimed Tom.

"Why?" asked all the others together.

"Because," he replied, "we have been such ever-
lasting idiots as to sail at night without showing a
light."

LIFTING THE BOAT OVER THE PILES.

## CHAPTER IX.

THE boat was in a shallow part of the river, between the shore and a long row of piles that marked the steamboat channel. Harry sounded with an oar, and found that the water was only two feet deep. "We'll have to get overboard and drag the boat over the piles," said he, "and it's going to be a mighty hard job, too. That swell threw us over as neat as the bull threw Joe over the fence up at Lenox last summer."

"When I got pitched over that fence I stayed there," said Joe. "I didn't try to get back into the field where the bull was, and I don't see what we want to get back where the steamboats are for."

"That's so," exclaimed Harry. "We're safe enough here. "Let's get the water out of the boat, and keep on this side of the piles."

7

When the boat was made dry, and the lighted lantern was hoisted to the top of the mast, Tom resumed his place at the helm, and Harry and Joe prepared to take another nap. "I don't want to grumble," said Joe, "but I wish I didn't have to lie on the coffee-pot and a tin cup. I don't feel comfortable on that kind of bed."

"I'll change with you if you like," replied Harry. "I'm sleeping on a beautiful soft bottle of oil, and some sardine boxes, but I don't want to be selfish and keep the best bed for myself."

"Oh, never mind," returned Joe. "I'll manage to sleep if Jim don't step on my face. I always did hate to have anybody step on my face when I was asleep."

"Well, good-night everybody," said Harry. "I'm going straight to sleep. Tom, be sure you wake me up if a steamboat tries to climb over these piles."

This time Tom did not fall asleep at the helm, but the wind gradually died away, and the sail hung limp and useless. Jim got out the oars without stepping on anybody, and rowed slowly on. In a little while they came to the end of the shallow lagoon into which the swell had so unexpectedly cast them. A sand-bank stretched from the shore to the line of piles, and it was impossible to go any farther. Tom decided to make the boat fast to the limb of a willow-tree that projected over the water, and to go ashore and sleep on the sand. Neither he nor Jim thought it worth while to wake the other boys; so they gathered up their blankets, crept quietly out of the boat, and were soon asleep on the soft, warm sand. When Harry and Joe awoke at daylight, stiff and cramped, they were disposed to be rather indignant at Tom and Jim, who were sleeping so comfortably on the sand; but Tom soon convinced them that he had acted from the best of motives, and they readily forgave him.

Of course breakfast was the first business of the day, and after that was finished the boat had to be entirely unloaded before she could be lifted over the piles into the channel. For the first time since they had started on the cruise the breeze was ahead, but it was so light that it was of very little consequence. The sky was cloudy, and the day promised to be a cool one; so the boys resolved to take to their oars and try, if possible, to reach Albany before night. When the boat was loaded, Tom and Jim each took a long oar, and Harry took his usual seat in the stern-sheets. They all felt fresh in spite of their night's adventure, and started gayly on their intended long day's row.

By this time they had found out that, although round tin boxes were very well to keep things dry, they are by no means handy to carry in a boat. Their shape made it impossible to stow them compactly. Joe, who sat at the bow, always had to pick his way over these tin boxes in going to or coming from his station; and he was constantly catching his foot in the spaces left between the boxes, and falling down on them. This smashed in the covers, and tried Joe's temper sorely. Once he sat down so violently on the box which held the sugar, that he went completely through the cover, and was fastened in the box as securely as a cork in a bottle. He was only released after a great deal of work, and just in time to enable the boys to have sugar in their coffee at night. Harry resolved that he would never cruise again with round boxes, but would have small rubber bags made, in which to put everything that required to be kept dry.

The boys took turns at the oars every hour, and rowed steadily until noon. They gave themselves an hour for lunch and resting, and then resumed their work. Late in the afternoon they came in sight of Albany, and went ashore, so as to get their dinner before reaching the city. After dinner they again pulled away at the oars, and at about nine o'clock they stopped at a lumber-yard on the outskirts of Albany, and, creeping in among the lumber, wrapped their blankets around them, and dropped asleep, completely worn out, but proud of their long day's row.

Before sunrise the next morning, Tom was awakened by a stick which was thrust into his ribs. Without opening his eyes, he muttered, "You quit that, or I'll get up and pound you!" and immediately dropped asleep again. Somebody then kicked him so sharply that he roused himself up, and, opening his eyes, was dazzled by the gleam of a bull's-eye lantern. He could not at first imagine where he was; but, as he presently found that a big policeman had him by the collar, and was calling him "an impudent young thief," he began to imagine that something was wrong.

"I've got you this time," said the policeman, "and the whole gang of you. Where did you steal that property in your boat from, you precious young river pirate?"

"We're not river pirates," replied Tom. "We're Moral Pirates, and we brought those things in the boat with us from New York."

"Well, I like your cheek!" said the officer; "owning up that you're pirates. Now just you and your gang take everything out of that boat and let me see what you've got. If any of you try to escape, I'll put a bullet into you. You hear me?"

The other boys had been awakened by the loud voice of the policeman, and were staring at him in utter astonishment.

"He thinks we're river thieves," said Tom. "Harry, we'll have to show him what we've got in the boat, and then he'll see his mistake."

Harry eagerly assured the policeman that they had come from New York on a pleasure cruise, and had nothing in the boat except provisions and stores. "That's a pretty story," said the officer. "You can tell that to the court. Your boat's full of junk that you've stolen from somewhere; and you'd better hand it out mighty quick!"

The boys were thus compelled to unload their boat, while the policeman stood over them with his club in one hand and his lantern in the other. He was not a stupid man, and he soon perceived that the boys had told him the truth; they were not the gang of river thieves for whom he had mistaken them. He therefore apologized, in a rough way, and even helped the boys repack the boat.

"What I can't understand," said he, "is why you boys come here and sleep in a lumber-yard, when you might be sleeping at home in your beds. Now if you were thieves, you couldn't get any better lodgings, you know; but you're gentlemen's sons, and you ought to know better. Why don't you go down to the hotel and live like gentlemen? Where's the fun in being arrested, and taking up my valuable time?"

The boys assured him that they had never enjoyed themselves more than they had while on the cruise, and after a little more talk the officer turned slowly away.

"By-the-bye," he exclaimed, suddenly turning back again, "one of you told me you were pirates. I ought to take you in after all. I believe you're a lot of boys that have been reading dime novels, and have run away from home."

"I didn't say we were pirates," replied Tom. "I

said we were Moral Pirates. That's a very different thing."

"Of course it is," said Joe. "A Moral Pirate is a sort of missionary, you know. I'm afraid you don't go to Sunday-school, officer, or you'd know better."

The policeman could not quite make up his mind whether Joe was in joke or in earnest; but as he could find no real reason for arresting the boys, he contented himself with telling them to leave the lumber-yard as soon as the sun rose. "And you'd better look out," he added, "that you don't come across any real river thieves. They'll make no bones of seizing your boat, and knocking you on the head if you make any noise." When he was fairly out of sight, the boys crept back to their shelter among the lumber, and coolly went to sleep again. They were so tired that neither policemen nor river thieves had any terrors for them.

## CHAPTER X.

THE policeman did not return, and the boys slept until an hour after sunrise. They then rowed down the river to the steamboat landing, where they left their boat in charge of a boatman and went to a hotel for breakfast. The waiters were rather astonished at the tremendous appetites displayed by the four sunburnt boys, and there is no doubt that the landlord lost money that morning. After breakfast Harry went to the express-office, where he found a large water-proof India-rubber bag, which the Department had sent in answer to his letter. At the post-office were letters from home for all the boys, and a postal order for ten dollars from Uncle John for the use of the expedition. Harry had no idea that this money would be needed, but it subsequently proved to be very useful.

Quite a quantity of stores were bought at Albany, for the voyage up the Hudson had lasted longer than any one had supposed it would, and the provisions were getting low. No unnecessary time was spent in buying these stores, for a fair wind was blowing, and all the boys were anxious to take advantage of it. By ten o'clock they were again afloat; and soon after noon they reached Troy and entered the canal.

The canal basin was crowded with canal-boats, and to avoid accidents the *Whitewing's* mast was taken down, and the oars were got out. Harry knew that, in order to pass through the locks, it would be necessary to pay toll, and to procure an order from the canal authorities directing the lock-men to permit the *Whitewing* to pass. The canal-boatmen, of whom he made inquiries, told him where to find the office, which was some little distance up the canal. When the office was reached, an officer came and inspected the boat, asked a great many questions about the cruise up the Hudson, and seem-

ed to be very much interested in the expedition.  He
told the boys that the water was low in the Champlain Canal, and that the lockmen might not be willing to open the locks for so small a boat; but that
they could avoid all dispute by entering the locks at
the same time with some one of the many canal-
boats that were on their way north.  He charged
the *Whitewing* the enormous sum of twenty - five
cents for tolls, and gave Harry an important-looking
order by which the lockmen were directed to allow
the skiff *Whitewing*, Captain Harry Wilson, to pass
through all the locks on the canal.

Thanking the pleasant officer, the boys pushed off.
After they had passed the place where the Champlain Canal branches off from the Erie Canal, they
were no longer troubled by a crowd of canal-boats,
and were able to set the sail again.  Unluckily, the
mast was just a little too high to pass under the
bridges, and at the first bridge which they met they
narrowly escaped a capsize—Jim succeeding in getting the mast down only just in time to save it from

GOING THROUGH THE LOCK.

striking the bridge. They had hardly set sail again when another bridge came in sight, and they could see just beyond it a third bridge. It would never do to stop at every bridge and unship the mast; so Harry went on shore, borrowed a saw from a cooper's shop, and sawed six inches off from the top of the mast, after which the bridges gave them no more trouble.

The boys were very much interested in passing the first lock. They slipped into the lock behind a big canal-boat, which left just room enough between its rudder and the gate for the *Whitewing.* When the lockmen shut the gate behind the boat, and opened the sluices in the upper gate, the water rose slowly and steadily. The sides of the lock were so steep and black that the boys felt very much as if they were at the bottom of a well; but it was not many minutes before the water had risen so high that the upper gates were opened, and the big canal-boat and its little follower were released.

Passing through a lock in a small boat, and in

company with a canal-boat, is not a perfectly safe thing to do; for if the ropes which fasten the canal-boat should break—which they sometimes do—the water rushing in through the sluices would force the canal-boat against the lower gate, and crush the small boat like an egg-shell. It is therefore best always to pass through a lock alone, or in company with other small boats. The danger, however, is in reality very slight, and very few accidents occur in canal locks.

The wind died away before sunset; and the boys having had only a light lunch, which they ate on the boat, were glad to go ashore for supper. They bought some corn from a farmer, and roasted it before the fire, while some nice slices of ham were frying, and the coffee-pot was boiling, and so prepared a supper which they greatly enjoyed. The moon came up before they had finished the meal, and they felt strongly tempted to make another attempt at night-work.

"I'll tell you what we can do," exclaimed Harry.

" Instead of rowing, let's tow the boat. One fellow can tow while another steers, and the rest can sleep in the boat."

" All right," said Joe. " I'm willing to be a mule. Only I'd like to know where my harness is coming from."

" We've got rope enough for that," replied Harry. " I'll take the first turn, and tow for an hour, while Joe steers; then I'll steer for an hour, while Joe tows. Then the other watch will take charge of the boat for two hours, and Joe and I will sleep."

" If I'm to sleep on the bottom of that boat," said Joe, " I want some nice sharp stones to sleep on. I'm tired of sleeping on coffee-pots, and want a change."

A long tow-line was soon rigged on Harry's shoulders in such a way that it did not chafe him; a space in the bottom of the boat was cleared of coffee-pots and other uncomfortable articles, and a pair of blankets was spread on the bottom board, so as to make a comfortable bed, which Tom and Jim hastened to occupy. Joe took the yoke-lines in his hand,

8

and called to Harry to go ahead. When Harry first tugged at the tow-line, the boat seemed very heavy; but as soon as she was in motion, Harry found that he could tow her as fast as he could walk, and with-out any difficulty.

Had the locks been open and the canal-boats been out of the way, the experiment of towing the *White-wing* at night would have been very successful. As it happened, the locks were kept closed during the night, because the water was low; and the canal-boats, not being able to pass the locks, were moored to the tow-path. These boats gave Harry and Joe a great deal of trouble. When one of them was met, Harry had to unharness himself and toss the rope into the boat, and Joe had to get out an oar and scull around the obstacle. This happened so often that Tom and Jim got very little sleep; and long before it was time for them to resume duty, a lock was reached, and Harry had to call all hands to drag the boat around it.

This was a·hard piece of work. First, all the

heavy things had to be taken out of the boat and carried around the lock. Then the boat had to be dragged out of the canal on to the tow-path; hauled up a steep ascent, and launched above the upper gate. It took a good half-hour to pass the first of these closed locks, and when the boat was again ready to start, it was time to change the watch.

Tom and Jim had managed to get only a few minutes' sleep, but Harry and Joe could not sleep a single wink. They had not "turned in" for more than ten minutes, when another lock was reached. This involved a second half-hour of hard work by all hands, and twenty minutes later three more locks close together blocked the way. It was foolish to persevere in dragging the boat around locks all night long; so, after getting her out of the canal on the side opposite to the tow-path, the boys dragged her behind some bushes, where the canal-boatmen could not see her at daylight. They then spread their rubber blankets on the ground, and prepared to sleep through the remaining four or five hours of darkness.

"Boys," said Joe, suddenly, "does it hurt a fat woman to jump on her?"

"Don't know," answered Harry. "What do you ask for?"

"Oh, nothing," said Joe. "Only when I was jumping from one canal-boat to another while I was a mule, I landed awfully heavy on a fat woman who was sleeping on deck."

"What did she do?" asked Harry.

"She didn't do anything. She just said, 'Go way wid you now, Pathrick,' as if she was half asleep and dreaming. Pathrick must be in the habit of jumping on her."

"Well, if she likes it, that's her business, not yours," suggested Harry. "Go to sleep, do!"

"I am going to sleep; but I don't think we ought to spend our nights in getting run down by steam-boats and jumping on strange fat women. I'm sure it isn't right. There, you needn't throw any more shoes at me! I won't say another word."

## CHAPTER XI.

"BOYS," said Tom, as he was kindling the fire the next morning, "do you know what day it is?"

"Saturday, of course," replied the others.

"You're wrong; it's Sunday."

"It can't be," exclaimed Harry.

"But it is," persisted Tom. "Last night was the sixth night that we've slept out-doors, and we started on a Monday."

Tom was right; but it was some time before his companions could convince themselves that it was actually Sunday. When they finally admitted that it was Sunday morning, they gave up the idea of proceeding up the canal, and began to discuss what they had better do,

928638A

The boat, which had been drawn out of the water the night before, was concealed by a clump of bushes from the canal-boatmen. The boys decided to leave it where it was, and to carry the tent and most of their baggage to a grove a quarter of a mile distant, where they could pass a quiet Sunday. The locks were not yet opened, and no canal-boats were stirring, and the boys made their way to the grove at once while their movements were unobserved. They were afraid that if they attracted the attention of the boatmen to the clump of bushes some one would steal the *Whitewing* while her crew were absent. They had already seen enough of the "canalers" to know that they were a wild and lawless set of men, and they were not anxious to put the temptation of stealing a nice boat in their way.

The grove was a delightful place; and when they had pitched the tent under the shadow of the great oak-trees, they were glad of the prospect of a good day's rest. Tom and Harry walked nearly a mile to church in the morning, leaving the Sharpe boys to look after the camp, and they all slept most of the afternoon.

About dusk, as the fire for cooking supper was blazing briskly, Joe returned from a foraging ex-dition, quite out of breath, and with his milk-pail half empty. He said that he had met three tramps on the road, which passed through the grove not very far from the camp, and that they had snatched a pie from him that he had bought at a farm-house, and had chased him for some distance.

He had been badly frightened, as he frankly admit-ted; but the other boys thought that it was a good joke on him. They told him that the tramps would track him by the milk that he had spilt, and would probably attack the camp and scalp him. They soon forgot the adventure, however, with the excep-tion of Tom; who, although he said nothing at the time, poured water on the fire as soon as the supper was cooked—an act which somewhat astonished the rest. Soon afterward he went into the tent for a few moments, and when he returned he was beginning to advise Joe not to laugh quite so loud, when the crackling of branches was heard in the grove, and three very unpleasant-looking men appeared.

It was fast growing dark, but Joe immediately recognized them as the tramps who had stolen his pie. "We've come to supper," said one of them. "Let's see what you've got. Give us the bill of fare, sonny, and look sharp about it."

Tom immediately answered that they had eaten their supper, and that there was nothing left of it but some coffee. "If you want the coffee, take it," said he. "There isn't anything else for you."

"That ain't a perlite way to treat three gen'lemen as come a long ways to call on you," said the tramp. "We'll just have to help ourselves, and we'll begin by looking into your tent. P'raps you've got a crust of bread there, what'll save a poor starvin' workin'-man from dyin' on the spot!"

Tom hastily stepped before the tent. "You can't go into this tent," he said, very quietly; "and you'd better leave this camp and go about your business."

"Just hear him," said the tramp, addressing his companions. "As if this yere identical camp wasn't our business. Now, boys," he continued, "you've got money with you, and you've got clothes, and one on you's got a watch, and you're goin' to give 'em to three honest hard-workin' men, or else you're goin' to have your nice little throats cut."

"Here, boys, quick!" cried Tom, rushing into the tent, where he was followed by the other boys before the tramps could stop them. "Here, Harry," he continued, "take the boat-hook. There's a hatchet for you, Jim, and a stick for Joe. Now we'll see if they can rob us!" So saying, he stepped outside the tent with the gun in his hand, followed closely by his little army.

The ruffians hesitated when they saw the cool way in which Tom confronted them. So they proposed a compromise, as they called it. "Look a here," said the one who had hitherto been the spokesman; "we ain't unreasonable, and we'll compromise this yere business. You give us your money and that chap's watch, and we'll let you alone. That's what I call a very handsome offer."

"We won't give you a thing," replied Tom; "and I'll shoot the first one of you that lays a hand on us."

The tramps consulted for a moment, and then the leader, with a frightful oath, ordered Tom to drop that gun instantly.

Tom never said a word, but he cocked both barrels and waited, with his eye fixed on the enemy.

Presently the tramps separated a little, the leader remaining where he had been standing, and the others moving one to the right and the other to the left of the boys. They evidently intended to rush on Tom from three directions at once, and so confuse him and prevent him from shooting.

"I'll take the leader and the man on the right," whispered Tom to Harry. "You lay for the other fellow with your boat-hook. I've given you fair warning," he continued, addressing the ruffians, "and I'll fire the minute you try to attack us."

The boys were standing close together in front of

THE FIGHT WITH THE TRAMPS.

the tent, Tom being a little in advance of the others. Suddenly the leader of the tramps called out, " Now then !" and all three made a rush toward Tom. He fired at the tramp in front of him, hitting him in the leg and bringing him to the ground ; but before he could fire again, the other two were upon him.

The boys gallantly stood by Tom. Harry attacked one of the tramps with the boat-hook so fiercely that the fellow cried out that he was stabbed, and ran away. Meanwhile Tom was struggling with the third tramp, who had thrown him down, and was trying to wrench the gun from him, while Jim and Joe were hovering around them afraid to strike at the tramp for fear of hitting Tom. But now Harry, having driven off his antagonist, flew to the help of Tom, and seizing the tramp by his hair, and bracing one knee against his back, dragged him backward to the ground, and held him there until Tom regained his feet, and, holding the muzzle of the gun at the robber's head, called on him to surrender, which the fellow gladly did.

"Get some rope, Jim, and tie him!" cried Tom. "Hold on to his hair, Harry, and I'll blow his brains out if he offers to move."

The tramp was not at all anxious to part with his brains, and he remained perfectly quiet while Jim and Joe tied his feet together, and his hands behind his back.

"Now you stand over him with the boat-hook, Harry," said Tom, "and I'll see to the other fellow."

The other fellow was, of course, the man who had been shot. Tom lighted the lantern, for it was now quite dark, and found that the ruffian had been shot in the lower part of his right leg, and had fainted from loss of blood. Taking a towel, Tom tore it into strips, and bound up the wound, and by the time he had finished the patient became conscious again, and begged Tom not to take him to prison.

Now this was precisely what the boys did not want to do, as it would probably delay them for several days, and perhaps put an end to their cruise. Tom therefore said to the prisoner, whom Harry was guarding, that if he would promise to help the wounded man away, and take him to see a doctor, he would be released. The tramp gladly accepted the offer, and Harry unfastened the rope from his legs and arms, while Tom kept his gun in readiness to use it at the first sign of treachery. The tramps, however, had quite enough of fighting, and were only too anxious to get away. The wounded man was helped to his feet by his companion, and the two went slowly off, one half carrying the other, and both cursing the coward who had run away. As they hobbled off, Tom called out, " I'm sorry I had to hurt you, but I couldn't help it, you know; and if any of you come back here to-night, you'll find us ready for you."

It was a long time before the boys fell asleep that night, and Tom was overwhelmed with praise for his coolness and bravery. Though he felt certain that the tramps would not return, he proposed that a sentinel should keep guard outside the tent, offering to share that duty with Harry, since the other boys were not familiar with guns. So all night long Tom and Harry, relieving one another every two hours, marched up and down in front of the tent, keeping a sharp watch for robbers, and preparing for a desperate fight every time they heard the slightest noise.

## CHAPTER XII.

THOUGH no tramps appeared during the night, the sentinels proved to be useful; for as soon as the day began to dawn, Harry, who was on sentry duty, called his comrades, and thus they were enabled to get breakfast early, and to start before six o'clock. They had to wait half an hour for the first lock to be opened, but after that they had no difficulty in passing through the other locks. They rowed steadily, taking turns at the oars, and occasionally fastening the boat to the stern of a canal-boat, which would tow them while they took a short rest. Early in the afternoon they reached Fort Edward, where they disembarked; and Harry and Tom went in search of a team, which they hired to carry them to Warrensburg, on the Schroon branch of the Hudson.

9

When the teamster drove down to the bank of the canal, Tom and the Sharpe boys began to unload the boat. Harry stopped them. "There isn't any use in taking the things out of the boat," said he. "We can draw her out of the canal and put her on the wagon just as she is."

"Her stern will dip under when we haul her bow out," said Tom.

"No it won't," replied Harry.

"Let's take the things out of the stern-sheets, any-how," urged Tom. "All our shoes are there, and we can't afford to lose them."

"Nothing will happen to them," answered Harry, confidently. "It's my boat, and I'm going to haul her out with the things in her."

Tom said no more, but took hold of the bow of the boat with the others, and they began to pull her out of the water. As Tom had prophesied, when she was about half-way out her stern dipped under, the water poured in, and nearly everything in the after-part of the boat floated out. The harm was done now, so the boys hastily dragged the boat up the bank, and then began to lament their losses.

There was not a shoe left, except the shoes that Harry and Tom had put on when they went in search of the team. The mast and sail and two oars were floating on the water, and a quantity of small articles, including the tin frying-pans and a tin pail, had shared the fate of the shoes, and were lying at the bottom of the canal.

"It was my fault," said Harry; "and I beg everybody's pardon. I'll strip and duck for the things till I find them." So saying, he threw off his clothes and sprang into the canal. Joe, who was, next to Harry, the best swimmer of the party, followed his example; and a number of the villagers and "canalers" collected on the tow-path to watch the divers.

The canal was not more than eight feet deep, but the bottom was very muddy, and the boys had to feel about in the mud with their feet for the lost articles. They were very fortunate, and before long succeeded in recovering all the shoes, except one of

Joe's, and several other things.   Meanwhile three women and half a dozen girls, all of whom lived on board the fleet of canal-boats that were lying near by, joined the spectators, and seemed to think that the whole business was a capital joke.   Harry and Joe were now anxious to come out of the water; but they could not come ashore while the women and girls were there, so they swam some distance up the canal, and crept out behind a barn.

Meanwhile Tom and Jim were busily baling out the boat, and arranging the wet things so that the sun could dry them.   They were so busy that they forgot all about Harry and Joe.   Presently Tom said, "Hark!  I think I hear somebody calling."

They listened, and presently they heard a voice in the distance calling, "Tom!  Jim!  boys!  somebody! Bring us our clothes!"

"It's Harry and Joe," exclaimed Tom.   "Where on earth are they?"

They looked up the canal, and finally discovered a naked arm waving frantically from behind a barn

HARRY AND JOE IN A TRAP.

that stood near the water. "They must be behind that barn," said Tom. "Why, the mosquitoes will eat 'em alive! I'll take their clothes to them right away." So saying, Tom gathered up the shirts, trousers, and hats of the two unhappy divers, and ran with them to their owners. He found Harry and Joe crouched behind the barn, chattering with cold and surrounded by clouds of eager mosquitoes. "We've been here half an hour," cried Joe, "and the mosquitoes would have finished us in another half-hour. I think my right leg is nearly gone already."

"And I know I must have lost a gallon of blood," said Harry.

"But why on earth did you come here?" asked Tom.

"Because the canal is just lined with women and girls," replied Joe. "They think it's a circus; but I'm not going to do circus-acting without tights."

The boys hurriedly dressed themselves, and returning to the boat helped to put it on the wagon;

and with the wet shoes hanging from the cart-rungs they started on their ride to Warrensburg. It was a hot and tedious ride, and as the wagon had no springs, the boys were bumped so terribly that they ached all over. They tried to sing, but the words were bumped out of them in the most startling way; and after singing one verse of the Star-spangled Banner in this fashion,

"The St-t-tar-spangl-led-led ba-a-an-na-na—"

they gave it up.

About four o'clock they reached Warrensburg, and after getting some dry sugar to replace that which had been mixed with canal water, they launched the boat and rowed up the river. They found it a narrow stream, with a rapid current and a good depth of water. After their tiresome ride the smooth motion of the boat seemed delightful, and they were really sorry when they found it was so late that they must camp for the night.

They chose a pleasant sandy spot between the

river and the edge of a thick wood. The opposite bank was also thickly wooded, and they felt as if they were in the depths of a wilderness; though, in reality, there were houses quite near at hand. They pitched their tent, made a good supper — of which they were in need, for they had eaten very little at noon—and then "turned in."

For some reason—perhaps because the mosquitoes had so cruelly maltreated him—Joe was not sleepy; and after having lain awake a long time while the other boys were sleeping soundly, he began to feel lonesome. He heard a great many mysterious noises, as any one who lies awake in a tent always does. The melancholy call of the loon sounded ghostly, and the sighing of the wind in the trees seemed to him like the breathing of huge animals. After awhile he found himself getting nervous as well as lonesome, and imagined that he saw shadows of strange objects passing in front of the tent. By-and-by he distinctly heard the twigs and branches crackling, as somebody or something moved through the woods. The noise came nearer, and suddenly it flashed upon Joe that a bear was approaching the tent. He crept carefully to the opening of the tent, and putting his head out, saw indistinctly a large animal moving slowly in the shadow of the bushes only three or four rods from the tent.

Joe lost no time in waking up the other boys, cautioning them as he did so not to make the least noise. "There's a bear close by the tent," he whispered. "I've been listening to him for a long while, and just now I saw him."

Harry immediately grasped the gun, both barrels of which he had loaded before going to sleep. Tom wished that he had the hatchet, but as it had been left in the boat, he had no weapon but his penknife. Thus armed, the two crept stealthily out of the tent to fight the bear, leaving Joe and Jim in a very unhappy state of mind, with nothing to defend themselves against the bear, in case he should attack the tent, except a tooth-brush and a lantern.

The outline of the animal could be seen, but Tom

and Harry could not make out which end of it was its head. "You must shoot him just behind the shoulder," whispered Tom. "That's the only spot where you can kill a bear." Harry said nothing, but watched carefully to see the animal move. Presently it threw up either its head or tail—the boys could not tell which—and started toward the tent. Harry forgot all about shooting at the shoulder, but in his excitement fired at the animal generally, without picking out any particular spot in which to plant his shot.

The effect of the shot was surprising. The bear set up a tremendous bellow, and by the flash of the gun the boys saw their dreaded enemy galloping away, with its horns and tail in the air. Tom burst into a loud laugh. "Come out, Joe," he cried. "Your bear's gone home to be milked—that is, if Harry hasn't mortally wounded her."

Fortunately, Harry had made a miss; and he found his whole charge of shot the next morning in the trunk of a big white birch-tree. The innocent cow that Joe had mistaken for a bear was, however, so thoroughly frightened that she did not come near the camp again.

"I stick to it that it was a bear!" said Joe, as the boys were wrapping themselves in their blankets. "Cows go to roost at sunset. Suppose it did bellow: how do you know that bears don't bellow when they are shot?"

"How about the horns, Joe?" asked Tom.

"There's horned owls — why shouldn't there be horned bears? Anyway, I believe it was a bear, and I shall stick to it." And to this day Joe believes—or thinks he does—that he had a very narrow escape from a ferocious bear on the banks of the Schroon.

## CHAPTER XIII.

THE cruise up the Schroon was a delightful one while it lasted. The river was so narrow that the trees on either side frequently met, forming a green and shady arch. Although there was a road not far from the river, and there were houses and small villages at a little distance from its banks, the boys while in their boat saw nothing but the water, the trees, and the sky, and felt as far removed from civilization as if they were sailing on an African river. They saw nothing to shoot, after their adventure with Joe's bear, and there were no signs of fish in the water; but they delighted in the wild and solitary river, and were very much disappointed when, at the close of the day, they reached a dam so high that it seemed hopeless to try to carry the boat around it.

Before camping they walked some distance above the. dam, and found that the river was completely blocked up with logs, which had been cut in the forest above and floated down to the saw-mill. The men at the mill said that the boys would find the river choked with logs for a distance of nearly three miles, and that a little farther up it became a mere brook, too shallow and rapid to be navigated with the *Whitewing*.

It was clear that the cruise on the Schroon had come to an end, and that it would be necessary to hire a wagon to take the boat to the lake. Having reached this decision, the boys made their camp; and being very tired, put off engaging a team until morning.

When morning came, one of the men at the mill came to see them while they were at breakfast, and advised them not to go to Schroon Lake. He said that the lake was full of houses—by which he meant that there were a great many houses along its banks —and that if they were to go there they would find neither shooting nor fishing. He urged them to go to another lake which they had never heard of before — Brandt Lake. It was no farther off than Schroon Lake, and was full of fish. Besides, it was a wild mountain lake, with only two or three houses near it. The boys thanked him, and gladly accepted his advice. They had supposed that Schroon Lake was in the wilderness, and were exceedingly glad to find out their mistake in time to select a more attractive place. The owner of the saw-mill furnished them with a wagon, and soon after breakfast they started for Brandt Lake.

When, after a pleasant ride, they came in sight of the lake, they were overjoyed to find how wild and beautiful it was. Steep and thickly wooded hills surrounded it, except at the extreme southern point, where they launched their boat. It was not more than two miles wide at the widest part, and was about five miles in length, and they could see but two houses—one on the east, and the other on the west shore. They eagerly hoisted the sail, and started up the lake to search for a permanent camp-ing-ground; and, after spending the afternoon in examining almost the entire line of shore, they selected a little rocky island in the upper part of the lake, which seemed made for their purpose.

There was a great deal of work to be done, for they intended to stay at Brandt Lake for a fortnight. They had to clear away the underbrush, and cut down several small trees to make room for the tent. Then a small landing-place had to be built of stones and logs, so that the boat could approach the island without striking on the sharp rocks which surrounded it. Then the stores were all to be taken out of the boat, and placed where they would be dry and easy of access. The provisions had by this time become nearly exhausted; but the boys had been told that they could get milk, eggs, butter, bread, and vegetables at one of the houses which was not more than a mile from the camp, so they were not troubled to find that of their canned provisions nothing was left except a can of peaches.

Of course all this work was not done in one day. On the afternoon of their arrival at the lake the boys merely pitched the tent, and then went fishing with a view to supper. Fishing with drop lines from a large rock at one end of their little island, they caught perch as fast as they could pull them in, good-sized pickerel, and two or three cat-fish. That night they ate a supper that would have made a boarding-house keeper weep tears of despair, and went to bed rather happier than they had ever felt before.

Tom was to row over to the house for milk and other provisions in the morning; but when morning came the boat was gone. She had broken loose during the night, not having been properly fastened, and had floated quietly away. A faint speck was visible on the surface of the lake about two miles away, which Harry, who had remarkably good eyes, said was the *Whitewing*. Whether he was right or wrong, it was quite certain that the boys were imprisoned on the island, with nothing to eat but a can of peaches and some coffee and sugar.

10

The fish, however, were waiting to be caught, and before very long a breakfast of fish and of coffee without milk was ready. The boys then began to discuss the important question of how they were to get back their boat, or to get away from the island.

It was a mile to the shore, and nobody felt able to swim that distance. Joe proposed that they fasten one of their shirts to a tall tree, as a signal of distress, and then fire the gun every minute. The objection to this plan was that the nearest house was out of sight behind a little point of land, and that no one would see the signal, or would understand why the gun was fired. Then Tom proposed to build a raft, on which two boys could paddle after the runaway boat. This was a practicable suggestion, and it was at once put into execution.

It was hard work to cut down timber enough to build a raft, but by perseverance the raft was finished before noon. It consisted of four logs laid side by side, and bound together with handkerchiefs, shoestrings, green twigs, and a few strips from one of

HARRY SETS OUT IN PURSUIT OF THE BOAT.

Harry's shirts, which he said was unnecessarily long. It was covered with two or three pieces of flat drift-wood; and when it was finished a piece of board was found which was shaped with the hatchet into a rude paddle. Then Tom and Harry proceeded to embark.

The raft floated Harry very well, but promptly sank when Tom also stepped on it. Either more timber must be added to it, or one boy must go alone in search of the boat. Harry insisted upon go-ing at once, and as the lake was perfectly smooth, and he could swim well, there did not seem to be great risk in his making the voyage alone. Bidding the boys good-bye, he paddled slowly away, and left his comrades to anxiously wait for his return.

It was ticklish work paddling the raft. The logs were fastened together so insecurely, owing to the fact that all the rope was in the runaway boat, that Harry was in constant fear that they would come apart, and was obliged to paddle very carefully to avoid putting any strain on the raft. With such a craft speed was out of the question; and after an hour of hard work the raft was only half-way between the island and the boat. Harry was not easily discouraged, however, and he paddled on, knowing that if nothing happened he must reach the boat in course of time.

Something did happen. When, after paddling for more than two hours, the *Whitewing* was rather less than a quarter of a mile from the raft, Harry missed a stroke with his paddle, and tumbled over. He struck the raft with his shoulder, and went through it as easily as if it had been fastened together with paper. When he came to the surface again he found that the raft had separated into its original logs, and that his voyage on it was ended. Luckily the *Whitewing* was now within swimming distance, so he struck out for her, and finally crept into her over the stern, so much exhausted that he had to lie down and rest before taking to the oars. Had the raft gone to pieces half an hour sooner he would have been in a dangerous position; for it is doubtful if he could have clung to one of the logs long enough to drift to the shore without becoming totally exhausted.

The boys on the island did not witness the end of Harry's raft, for it was too far away when the accident occurred for them to see anything but a little black dot on the water. They became, however, very anxious about him as the hours went by and he did not come back. Tom was especially uneasy, and blamed himself for permitting Harry to go alone. He thought of making another raft and going in search of Harry; but there were no more strings with which to fasten logs together, and he did not quite like to tear up his clothes and use them for that purpose. He did, however, resolve that, if Harry did not come in sight within another hour, he would take a small log and, putting it under his arms, try to swim to the main-land and borrow a boat, if one could be found, in which to search for his comrade. He was spared this hazardous experiment; for toward the end of the afternoon Harry and

the *Whitewing* came in sight, and were welcomed
with a tremendous cheer.

Tom took the boat and went for provisions, and
when he returned the *Whitewing* was not only dragged on shore, but fastened to two different trees with
two distinct ropes.  The boys were determined that
she should not escape again; and when Joe proposed
that somebody should sit up with her all night, so
that she could not cut the ropes and run away, Tom
seriously considered the proposal.  The next day a
snug little dock was built, in which she seemed quite
contented, and from which she could not escape without climbing over a stone breakwater — a feat of
which there was no reason to believe that she was
capable.

## CHAPTER XIV.

THE boys had been on their island for more than a week when they resolved to make an excursion to Schroon, which was the nearest village, in order to get some sugar, coffee, and other necessaries. Schroon Lake, or rather the lower end of it, was not more than five miles from Brandt Lake; but there was a range of high hills between the two, and the village of Schroon was situated at the head of the lake, which was nearly ten miles in length. A long and tiresome journey was, therefore, before them, and they ought to have started early in the morning; but they did not start until nearly eleven o'clock. Harry, Tom, and Joe were to go to Schroon together, and Jim was to stay at the island until six o'clock, when he was to row over to the west shore and bring the others back to the camp.

When they bade good-bye to Jim, the three other boys assured him that they would certainly be back as early as six o'clock, and warned him not to fail to meet them with the boat. They then started to cross the hills, following a foot-path, that was so little used that it was hardly visible. Unfortunately the path led through a thicket of raspberry bushes, and the fruit was so tempting that the boys lost a good deal of time by stopping to gather it. After a tiresome tramp under the mid-day sun they reached the lower end of Schroon Lake, where they hired a crank little row-boat, and rowed up to Schroon. There was a fresh northerly breeze which delayed them; and the spray from the bow of the boat sprinkled them, so that they were uncomfortably wet when they reached the village. By this time they were very hungry as well as tired, and so they went to the hotel for dinner. It was half-past six o'clock when they started to row down the lake,

BIDDING JIM GOOD-BYE.

and several men who saw them warned them that they were running a good deal of risk in attempting to return at so late an hour.

The trip down the lake was certainly a rather foolhardy one; for there was a good deal of wind and sea, and long before they reached the landing-place it was quite dark. But the boys were anxious to get back to their camp, and for the first time during the cruise they acted somewhat recklessly. However, they met with no accident; and when they had returned the boat to its owner, they set out to cross the hills.

The path was not easy to find in the daylight, and it was next to impossible to find it in the night. A dozen times the boys lost themselves, and were compelled to depend entirely upon the stars to direct their course. The woods had been all cleared away for a space of a mile or a mile and a half wide between the two lakes, except just along the shore of Brandt Lake; so that it was not absolutely necessary for them to keep in the path, as it would have been had they been passing through a thick forest. Still it was not pleasant to lose the path, and stumble over stones and stumps, and of course it made the journey longer. They must have walked at least seven or eight miles on their way back before they finally reached their own lake at midnight, at the point where they expected to find Jim waiting for them.

Neither Jim nor the boat was there. He had waited until ten o'clock, and then, making up his mind that they had decided to spend the night at Schroon, he rowed back to the island, and went calmly to bed. An hour later a dense fog settled over the lake; and when the tired boys reached the shore they could see but a few yards in front of their eyes.

It was a terrible disappointment, but Harry tried to be cheerful. "We shall have to stay here to-night, boys," said he; "but we will build a good fire and keep warm." Tom said that he thought that was the best thing to do, for without a fire they would suffer severely from the cold, wet fog, and he asked Harry if he had any matches. Harry had none, Joe had none, and Tom had none; so the plan of building a fire came to nothing.

The cold gradually chilled them as they stood talking over their adventure, and their teeth began to chatter. Joe said he wished he could get hold of Jim for about five minutes, so that he could warm himself up by convincing him that he ought not to have taken the boat back to the island. Harry said nothing; but he was wondering whether he would freeze to death in the fog, and tried to remember how travellers overtaken by the snow on the Alps contrive to fight off the terrible drowsiness that steals over them when they are freezing. Tom was more practical. He did not expect to freeze in July, although he was miserably cold; and he did not want to punish Jim for a mistake of judgment. He knew that the house where they were accustomed to get milk was not far off, and that a boat usually lay on the shore near the house; so he proposed to Harry and Joe to borrow the boat and make their way into the camp.

"If we go to that house at this time of night, we shall get shot," remarked Harry. "The man is an ugly-tempered chap, and I heard him say the other day that if he ever heard anything prowling around the house at night, he always fired at it."

"Then we won't ask him for his boat: we'll borrow it without leave, and Jim can bring it back in the morning," replied Tom.

"This is nice conduct for Moral Pirates," said Joe. "Capturing a vessel at night is real piracy, and when Jim takes the boat back the man will be sure to shoot him. I'm sorry for Jim; but I hope it will be a warning to him not to leave his friends in such a fix that they've either got to borrow a boat without leave, or freeze."

They made their way stealthily and with great difficulty to the place where the boat lay. It was high and dry on the beach, and though the fog hid the house where the owner of the boat lived, the boys knew that it was very near. They launched the boat with the utmost caution, lest any noise should awaken the bad-tempered man with the shot-gun. They had it almost launched, when Harry's foot slipped on a wet stone, and he fell with a dismal crash, clinging to the boat, and dragging Tom and Joe down with him.

It was very certain that if anything could wake the owner of the boat, he must be awake by this time; so the boys sprang up, and shoving the boat into the water regardless of the noise, seized the oars, and rowed away into the fog. When they had gained what they thought a safe distance from the shore they ceased rowing, and congratulated themselves that they were all right at last. To be sure, Harry had scraped his ankle badly; Tom had forgotten the coffee, and left it on the shore; and Joe had put the sugar in the bottom of the leaky boat, where it was rapidly dissolving into sirup; but they were once more afloat, and expected to reach their comfortable camp within the next twenty minutes.

There was not a particle of air stirring, and not a star was visible, so they had absolutely nothing to steer by. They could not even hear the sound of the water which ordinarily lapped the shore. Still they were not discouraged. Harry thought he knew which way the camp lay, and so he and Tom rowed in what they imagined was the right direction.

They rowed for two hours without finding the island, and without reaching the shore. They could not understand it. The lake seemed to have grown in the night, and to have reached the size of Lake Ontario. They knew that by daylight they could row across it at its widest part in less than an hour, but now it seemed impossible to find any shore. Joe had just suggested that they had made a mistake in coming back from Schroon, and had walked all the way to Lake Champlain, on which they were now rowing, when the bow of the boat struck the shore.

It was some consolation to know that the lake actually had a shore; but they could not tell what part of the shore they had reached. They pushed off again, and resumed their hopeless search for the camp. A new trouble now harassed them. From seeming to have no shore at all, the lake now seemed to have shrunk to a mere mud-puddle. No matter in what direction they rowed, they would strike the shore within ten minutes, and always at a different place. Joe said that he had never dreamed that so much shore and so little lake could be put together.

Toward morning Harry and Tom became too tired to row, and they lay down in the bottom of the wet boat, and tried to keep warm by lying close to each other. Joe took the oars, and tried to row without hitting the shore; but he had hardly dipped his oars when the bow grated on the pebbles. He promptly gave up the attempt, and making the boat fast to a tree, joined Tom and Harry, and shared their misery.

They were much too cold and wretched to sleep, but they managed to keep from growing positively stiff with cold. The sun rose, but it did not for a long time make any impression on the fog. All at once, about seven o'clock, the fog vanished; and the boys found themselves in a little bay near the ex-treme northerly part of the lake. They had been rowing across this little bay, first in one direction and then in another, during all those miserable hours when they found such an unaccountable quan-tity of shore.

Of course they rowed down to the camp, where they found Jim still sleeping soundly, with a content-ed, happy look that was awfully exasperating. They woke him up, and scolded him with all the strength they had left, and then, putting on dry clothes, "turn-ed in," and slept all day. Jim towed the borrowed boat back, but was not shot; and the boys afterward said that, on the whole, they were rather glad that he still lived, and that they would mercifully forgive him.

## CHAPTER XV.

HERE was only one fault to be found with Brandt Lake; there was hardly anything to shoot in its vicinity. Occasionally a deer could be found; but at the season of the year when the boys were at the lake it was contrary to law to kill deer. It was known that there were bears in that part of the country as well as lynxes—or catamounts, as they are generally called; but they were so scarce that no one thought of hunting them. Harry did succeed in shooting three pigeons and a quail, and Tom shot a gray squirrel; but the bears, deer, catamounts, and ducks that they had expected to shoot did not show themselves.

On the other hand, they had any quantity of fishing. Perch and cat-fish swarmed all around the island; and large pickerel, some of them weighing six or eight pounds, could be caught by trolling.  Two miles farther north was another lake that was full of trout, and the boys visited it several times, and found out how delicious a trout is when it is cooked within half an hour after it is taken out of the water. In fact they lived principally upon fish, and became so dainty that they would not condescend to cook any but the choicest trout, and the plumpest cat-fish and pickerel.

It must be confessed that there was a good deal of monotony in their daily life.  In the morning somebody went for milk, after which breakfast was cooked and eaten.  Then one of the boys would take the gun and tramp through the woods in the hope of finding something to shoot, while the others would either go fishing or lie in the shade.  Once they devoted a whole day to circumnavigating the lake in the boat, and another day a long rain-storm kept them inside of the tent most of the time.  With these exceptions one day was remarkably like another; and at the end of two weeks they began to grow a little tired of camping, and to remember that there were ways of enjoying themselves at home.

Their final departure from their island camp was caused by an accident. They had decided to row to the southern end of the lake and engage a team to meet them the following week and to carry them to Glenn's Falls, where they intended to ship the boat on board a canal-boat bound for New York, and to return home by rail. To avoid the heat of the sun, they started down the lake immediately after break-fast, and forgot to put out the fire before they left the island.

After they had rowed at least a mile, Tom, who sat facing the stern, noticed a light wreath of smoke rising from the island, and remarked, "Our fire is burning yet. We ought not to have gone off and left it."

Harry looked back, and saw that the cloud of smoke was rapidly increasing.

"It's not the fire that's making all that smoke!" he exclaimed.

"What is it, then?" asked Tom.

"Perhaps it's water," said Joe. "I always thought that where there was smoke there must be fire; but Harry says it isn't fire."

"I mean," continued Harry, "that we didn't leave fire enough to make so much smoke. It must have spread and caught something."

"Caught the tent, most likely," said Tom. "Let's row back right away and put it out."

"What's the use?" interrupted Jim. "That tent is as dry as tinder, and will burn up before we can get half-way there."

"We must get back as soon as we can," cried Harry. "All our things are in the tent. Row your best, boys, and we may save them yet."

The boat was quickly turned, and headed toward the camp. The fire was rapidly increasing, and it was apparent that the dry underbrush must have caught; in which case the fire would soon fasten on the trees, and sweep over the whole of the little island.

THE EXPLOSION IN CAMP.

"There's one reason why I'm not particularly anxious to help put that fire out," Joe remarked, as they approached the island, and could see that a really alarming fire was in progress.

"What's that?" asked Harry.

"As near as I can calculate, there must be about two pounds—"

He was interrupted by a loud report from the island, and a shower of pebbles, sticks, and small articles—among which a shoe and a tin pail were recognized—shot into the air.

—"Of powder," Joe continued, "in the flask. I thought it would blow up, and now that it's all gone I don't mind landing on the island."

"Everything must be ruined!" exclaimed Jim.

"Lucky for us that we put on our shoes this morning," Tom remarked, as he rowed steadily on. "That must have been one of my other pair that just went up. I remember I put them in the corner of the tent close by the powder."

When they reached the island they could not at

first land, on account of the heat of the flames; but they could plainly see that the tent and everything in it had been totally destroyed. After waiting for half an hour the fire burnt itself out, so that they could approach their dock and land on the smoking ash heap that an hour before had been such a beautiful, shady spot. There was hardly anything left that was of any use. A tin pan, a fork, and the hatchet were found uninjured; but all their clothing and other stores were either burnt to ashes or so badly scorched as to be useless. Quite overwhelmed by their disaster, the boys sat down and looked at one another.

"We've got to go home now, whether we want to or not," Harry said, as he poked the ashes idly with a stick.

"Well, we meant to go home in a few days anyway," said Tom; "so the fire hasn't got very much the better of us."

"But I hate to have everything spoiled, and to have to go in this sort of way. Our tin pans and fishing-tackle aren't worth much, but all our spare clothes have gone."

"You've got your uncle's gun in the boat, so that's all right," suggested Tom, encouragingly. "As long as the gun and the boat are safe, we needn't mind about a few flannel shirts and things."

"But it's such a pity to be driven away when we were having such a lovely time," continued Harry.

"That's rubbish, Harry," said Joe. "We were all beginning to get tired of camping out. I think it's jolly to have the cruise end this way, with a lot of fireworks. It's like the transformation scene at the theatre. Besides, it saves us the trouble of carrying a whole lot of things back with us."

"The thing to do now," remarked Tom, "is to row right down to the outlet, and get a team to take us to Glenn's Falls this afternoon. We can't sleep here, unless we build a hut, and then we wouldn't have a blanket to cover us. Don't let's waste any more time talking about it."

"That's so! Take your places in the boat, boys,

and we'll start for home." So saying, Harry led the way to the boat, and in a few moments the *White-wing* was homeward bound.

The boys were lucky enough to find a man who engaged to take them to Glenn's Falls in time to catch the afternoon train for Albany. They stopped at the Falls only long enough to see the *Whitewing* safely on board a canal-boat, and they reached Albany in time to go down the river on the night boat.

After a supper that filled the colored waiters with astonishment and horror, the boys selected arm-chairs on the forward deck, and began to talk over the cruise. They all agreed that they had had a splendid time, in spite of hard work and frequent wettings.

"We'll go on another cruise next summer, sure," said Harry. "Where shall we go?"

Tom was the first to reply. Said he, "I've been thinking that we can do better than we did this time."

"How so?" asked the other boys.

"The *Whitewing* is an awfully nice boat," Tom continued, "but she is too small. We ought to have a boat that we can sleep in comfortably, and without getting wet every night."

"But, then," Harry suggested, "you couldn't drag a bigger boat round a dam."

"We can't drag the *Whitewing* round much of a dam. She's too big to be handled on land, and too little to be comfortable. Now, here's my plan."

"Let's have it," cried the other boys.

"We can hire a cat-boat about twenty feet long, and she'll be big enough, so that we can rig up a canvas cabin at night. We can anchor her, and sleep on board her every night. We can carry mattresses, so we needn't sleep on stones and stumps—"

—"And coffee-pots," interrupted Joe.

—"And we can take lots of things, and live comfortably. We can sail instead of rowing; and though I like to row as well as the next fellow, we've had a little too much of that. Now we'll get a cat-boat next summer, and we'll cruise from New

*The Moral Pirates.*

York Bay to Montauk Point. We can go all the way through the bays on the south side, and there are only three places where we will have to get a team of horses to drag the boat across a little bit of flat meadow. I know all about it, for I studied it out on the map one day. What do you say for that for a cruise?"

"I'll go," said Harry.

"And I'll go," said Jim.

"Hurrah for the cat-boat!" said Joe. "We can be twice as moral and piratical in a sail-boat as we can in a row-boat, even if it is the dear little *White-wing.*"

**THE END.**

www.ingramcontent.com/pod-product-compliance
Lightning Source LLC
Chambersburg PA
CBHW031115020726
47495CB00007B/2214